JULIUS WINSOME

JULIUS WINSOME

A NOVEL

Gerard Donovan

THE OVERLOOK PRESS

Woodstock & New York

This edition first published in the United States in 2006 by
The Overlook Press, Peter Mayer Publishers, Inc.
Woodstock & New York

WOODSTOCK:
One Overlook Drive
Woodstock, NY 12498
www.overlookpress.com
[for individual orders, bulk and special sales, contact our Woodstock office]

NEW YORK:
141 Wooster Street
New York, NY 10012

Library of Congress Cataloging-in-Publication Data

Donovan, Gerard, 1959-
Julius Winsome : a novel / Gerard Donovan.
p. cm.
1. Pets—Death—Fiction. 2. Hunters—Fiction.
3. Grief—Fiction. 4. Revenge—Fiction. I. Title.
PR6054.O557J85 2006   823'.914—dc22   2006048285

Book design and type formatting by Bernard Schleifer
Manufactured in the United States of America
ISBN-10 1-58567-849-X / ISBN-13 978-1-58567-849-5
10 9 8 7 6 5 4 3 2 1

for Doug Swanson and
Christina Nalty

Those who live the longest and those who die the soonest lose the same thing. The present is all that they can give up, since that is all you have.

—MARCUS AURELIUS

PART ONE

October 30th-November 2nd

1

I THINK I HEARD THE SHOT.

It was a cold afternoon at the end of October, and I was in my chair reading by the wood stove in my cabin. In these woods many men roam with guns, mostly in the stretches away from where people live, and their shots spray like pepper across the sky, especially on the first day of the rifle hunting season when people from Fort Kent and smaller towns bring long guns in their trucks up this way to hunt deer and bear.

But the metal punch that rang across the forest seemed a lot closer, less than a mile off if it's the sound that killed him, but the truth is that I have imagined hearing it so many times since, rewound the tape of those moments so often, that I cannot tell anymore the true sound of the rifle from the phantom of my thoughts.

That was close, I said, and opened the woodstove and shoved in another log, closing it before the smoke poured out and filled the room.

Most of the hunters, even the beginners, kept to the open forest, farther west in the North Maine Woods and to the Canadian border, but a good rifle carries far, and the distance can be tricky to figure without walls and roads.

It still sounded too close. The seasoned hunters knew where I lived and where all the cabins were in the woods, some in the open, some hidden. They knew not to discharge a weapon, that bullets will travel until they hit something.

I had a good fire going and my legs were warm, and I finished the short story by Chekhov where a girl cannot sleep and the baby won't stop crying, and was so caught up in it that I didn't notice my dog was gone. I had let him out a few minutes before and it was nothing new for him to wander off, though mostly he stayed a hundred yards or so from the cabin in a big circle, his territory, the thing he owned.

I went to the door and called for him, thinking again that the sound was a bit close to the house, and then I checked again ten minutes later and still couldn't find my dog, he didn't come in when I called, louder each time, and when I walked to the edge of the woods and whistled, cupped my hands around my mouth and shouted, there was no sign, no brown shape breaking out of the undergrowth toward me as he always did when summoned.

The wind was cold and I closed the door and slid the towel on the floor against it to block the draft. Then I did something I rarely do in the winter months: I checked the clock.

It was four minutes past three.

2

NOVEMBER ARRIVES IN NORTHERN MAINE ON A COLD wind from Canada that knifes unfiltered through the thinned forest, drapes snow along the river banks and over the slope of hills. It's lonely up here, not just in fall and winter but all the time; the weather is gray and hard and the spaces are long and hard, and that north wind blows through every space unmercifully, rattling the syllables out of your sentences sometimes.

I grew up in these woods, the forest land at the western edges of the St. John Valley that borders the Canadian province of New Brunswick and runs along the banks and south of the St. John River with its rolling hills and small, back settlement towns. My grandfather was French Acadian, as was my mother, and for reasons unknown to me he built the cabin miles away from the French, on tree-covered land close to where the great woods began in the western part of the valley. At the time it was even more remote than now, and strange because those people stuck together: most who lived in those settlement towns were descended

from the French Acadians expelled by the British from
Nova Scotia in 1755. Some went south to Louisiana,
the rest moved eventually to Northern Maine, these
people of extremes, my father said, people of far south
and north.

It was strange also because of the winters. He built
the cabin on two acres of cleared land, with the woods
on all sides, and my father added a large barn, bigger
than the cabin, where he kept all his tools and the truck
and anything fragile or easily lost that would not survive the six winter months outside. The woods that
ringed the house were formed of evergreens and leaf-
shedders both—pines, oak, spruce, hemlock, maple—
and so the trees circling the cabin seemed to step back,
retreat in pieces as the leaves turned yellow and deep
rust, shredding off like dead skin as September came,
crinkling yellow along the floor of the woods as
October arrived, and blowing away into November.

The cabin came from my mother's French side,
my father being English, and I inherited it through her
by way of him. He told me that I wouldn't believe it if
I saw it, that the valley was like the rolling midlands of
England, but the tongue that echoed in these hills was
French, not English. And that was another strange decision, an Acadian woman marrying English, but she was
her own woman I am told, and anyway they are not
people you tell what to do.

The cabin blends into the woods, or the woods
into the cabin. One moment you are in forest stepping

over a branch, the next step puts you walking across a porch, and you want to be careful. Many men live in these woods who cannot live anywhere else; they live alone and are tuned close to any offense you might give them, best to keep your manners about you, and even better to have nothing to say at all. They come up north and wait out life, or they were here anyway and stayed for the same reason. Such men live at the end of all the long lanes in the world, and in reaching a place like this they have run out of country they can't live in. They have no choice but to build, and so they go as far out of the way as they can even here, in the deep shade of the trees. I lived far from the nearest of them, the closest cabins three miles to the west and north of me.

In summer I kept a bed of flowers along the edge of the clearing, about thirty feet by three, filled with nasturtiums, marigolds, lilies, and foxglove, and every year I added to the small lawn with sown grass that grew to a hot green carpet in the summer where I could lie down and smell the flowers and taste the blue sky. But this winter had come late; we had a strange, warmer south wind for most of October, and some of the flowers were still alive with their smell, way past season. I'd covered them with black plastic bags pulled out to little tents on poles to keep them alive through the odd night frost, hoping to keep their color another week and shorten the gray months ahead. They had made my life bright in summer and I wanted to help them. But in the last couple of days the temperatures had fallen, and soon these survivors would retreat too, find the safety of the soil and sleep in their seed under the vice-grips of deep winter.

Except for my dog I lived on my own, for I had never married, though I think I came near once, and so even the silences here were mine. It was a place built around silences: my father was a reader of books, and spreading along the walls from the wood stove stretched the long bookcases from the living room and on to the kitchen at the back and right and left to both bed-rooms, four shelves high, holding every book he ever owned or read, which was the same thing, for my father did indeed read everything. I was surrounded therefore by 3,282 books, leatherbound, first editions, paperbacks, all in good condition, arranged by alphabet and record-ed on lists written in fountain pen. And because the bookcase ringed the entire cabin—and since some rooms were darker and colder than others, being distant from the woodstove—there were also warm novels and cold novels. Many of the cold novels had authors whose last names began with letters after "J" and before "M," so writers like Johnson and Joyce, Malory and Owen lived back near the bedrooms. My father called it an outpost of Alexandria in Maine, after the Greek library, and he liked nothing better when he came in after work than to stretch his socks to the fire until they steamed, and in his thick sweater and smoking his pipe then turn to me and ask for a particular book, and I remembered the cold pages in my hands, carrying to my father the volume he wanted, watching it warm under his eyes by the fire, and when he was finished I carried the warm book back to its shelf and slid it in, a tighter fit because it had grown slightly in the heat.

Although he was gone for twenty years I had the novels and travel books, plays and short stories, all as he had left them, everything he was and knew still around me.

In the afternoon of that Monday I took one of those books to read, some Russian stories, and when I finished the story I strained a look out the window. Still no dog.

The clock again: Twenty minutes past three.

3

I WALKED INTO THE CLEARING AND SHOUTED.

Hobbes!

I hoped to see him run up behind me or jump out of the truck where he often slept during the day on the seat, where the windshield gathered the sunlight into a greenhouse, but another three shouts didn't bring him. To get my mind off him I took more logs from the woodpile and stacked them by the door. A small knot draped loosely in my stomach and lay there even though I ignored it and selected another book from the shelves and sat by the window. An essay by Alexander Pope in a first edition, published in 1757 in London, one of ten volumes bound in their original leather, the catalogue index card inside the cover. No good. I could not lose myself in the detail, and what would have once given me pleasure seemed so many loose and tedious words in my mind, the pain of stones: "The Works of Alexander Pope Esq. In 10 vols. London: printed for A. Millar, Jan R. Tonson, H. Lintot, and C. Bathurst, 1757. With frontispiece and twenty-three engraved plates, separate title-pages to each volume printed in red and black, in contemporary mottled calf, red morocco labels on spines lettered in gilt."

In the end I closed the book and sighed because the minutes joined at each side to pull the knot tighter.

The shot was too close, sounded wider than a rifle too. I replayed it and figured less than five hundred yards.

At forty minutes past three I walked to the edge of the woods again and cupped my hands and shouted his name. I heard the echo bounce off ahead like a skimming flat stone. Then I walked farther into the woods along a trail, a hundred yards, two hundred yards, and called again. It would soon be dark; this was the time when the deer came out. He may have seen one and ran after it, a pursuit that might take him two or three miles away. Often when I was out walking with him I'd see him dash off after a big buck without a hope of catching it, and I'm not sure what Hobbes would have done if he ever did catch up, and he was always back at the house before I was, waiting with his wagging tail and a parched mouth.

Since the hunting season had begun I tied an orange scarf around his neck as a sign to hunters, but it got torn off and I had not replaced it, something I regretted now as I made my way back. No use walking any more and fumbling my way along in the night.

At five minutes to four I arrived in the clearing and saw him lying in the flowers, bleeding, breathing, but barely. His eyes were open and he raised his head when he heard me. I ran to him and saw the wound, a shotgun.

He was still breathing when I got him to the veterinarian's office in Fort Kent, a fifteen-mile drive, the first three miles along a dirt road and overhanging trees. I swung around potholes, holding him steady and keeping pressure on the wound, saying his name to let him hear a word he knew, felt the damp on my hand. I sped up as I reached the paved road to the town. The doctor was dressed in his white coat having dinner in his kitchen when I knocked on the door. His wife answered it, holding her hand to her eyebrows under the porch bulb while she looked me up and down.

My dog's been shot, I said.

She looked to the truck with the door open idling in the driveway, saw Hobbes lying on the bench in the light. She clutched her collar and nodded, called to her husband.

A dog's been shot.

I appreciated the brevity of what she said. This was a woman who knew the value of seconds. The doctor ran out and we carried the dog to his office, which was attached to the house, and laid him on the metal bench.

He was shot up close, he said.

I told him I could see that already.

No, it was very close, the vet said, inches. The buckshot is well into his back.

You mean the gun was touching him, I said.

The person knew the dog, patted him first maybe, to get him that close, he said.

Then the doctor said I should go with his wife because he worked better on his own. I asked about staying for the dog to see someone he knew, but he shook his head and said again for me to go.

His wife brought me to the kitchen and gave me a cup of tea and told me not to worry. She was a good woman and I liked her; I remembered her kindness to my father when he made the long trip with another dog, twenty years and more before, shortly before his own death. She recognized me now, I could see.

You're Julius Winsome, she said.

I nodded.

He must have run after a deer to get so far from the house, I said.

They'll do that, she said. Poor thing.

Or gone for a walk, his nose in the air, I said.

She said, They like to go for walks, just like humans.

A bell sounded and she said that we should go back next door. As we walked in, all I could see were bandages and blood. He had lost so much blood.

You have to be mighty cruel and then some to pull the trigger on a dog like that, the doctor said, and he moved until his hand was on my shoulder, and I knew what he was saying. They left and I heard his wife ask him how things were and why couldn't he save him. His answer was gone as they closed the door and I stood there with my dog under the single light.

The little fellow looked at me and I held his head, and he lay his head on my arm and stopped breathing, as if he could let go like that, now that I was there.

4

IN TRUTH IT WAS A LONG WAY BACK TO THE CABIN. Hobbes lay beside me but I moved his head onto my lap for whatever comfort might be got for him even at this late stage. He had lost much of the heat from his body and the blood matted in his fur and the seat. That same night, shortly after getting back to the cabin, I ran the truck lights and buried him in the flower beds at the spot where I found him, a part I would see from the window when I looked out. It was hard to throw that first shovel of clay over his face, to see a hole gouged around the body that had so often ran after toys I'd thrown or shivered in dreams on the floor as he ran and barked. The shovel worked in and out of the light beams as the dirt hit him in the stomach, on his back, fell into his ears, his eyes, as I covered him along with the things that had made him: his walks, his rest, his eating when hungry, the stars he watched sometimes, the first day I brought him home, the first time he saw snow, and every second of his friendship, what he took with him into silence and stillness; I shoveled the whole world on top of my friend and felt the weight of it as though I lay with him in that dark.

After he was gone, I put the shovel in the barn and walked to the warm cabin and left him to stiffen. It rained that night, and it was cold after the fire went down. I lay in bed on Monday night listening to the wind whip around the house like a rope.

5

I WOKE ON TUESDAY MORNING TO A SPLINTER OF LIGHT
through the window, the first time the sun did not rise
on a living Hobbes. His grave was twenty feet from the
cabin, too close not to notice even if you tried to walk
past, and I couldn't bring myself to go outside and see
it, so I fumbled around inside the dark walls, walking
down the lines of books, plucking them out from their
tight positions along the shelves and dusting them in
the shaft of light through the front window until the air
filled with dust swirling in the morning rays; then I
went into the spare room and pulled two boxes from
under the bed, both marked "Alexandria," and found
inside them stacks of cards carefully wrapped in brown
elastic bands.

My father had indeed lined the house with 3,282
books, far too many for anyone to remember, and so he
drew up an index card for each one, listing author, pub-
lisher, and year, as well as a summary of contents. I
remembered the scratch of his fountain pen as he sat in
his antique New England chair, still there by the fire,

and scanned each cover up and down, over and under his spectacles, noting the details, moving his head from side to side, mumbling those details as he wrote. The fountain pen scratched through snow and spring, rain and fall. I stayed in the room, bent over the box, as the image of him flooded me like a running stream in woods after rainfall: how he sat straight in that green wool sweater he wore, his cashmere scarf, vaguely tinted with aftershave, covering his neck when it got cold even with a fire, and how I stayed close to him and read too, the silences stretching like vines through the cabin, broken only as each of us got up to make tea or cut some bread and butter. He was a gentle man and easy to live with because he took up very little room around him. Some people are like that, though very few, and it was from him I learned how to be still. We had lived alone together: he never remarried. He said there was only one woman for him, even if she had died, and from that I learned what loyalty is when you take the bare word that's written and put flesh on it and let it live.

After two pots of tea and with the fire already burning on its embers I glanced at the clock for the third time in two days, the most times that clock had been looked at in two months at least. Only noon. I had to get wood or the place would be frozen by three. It was the time of year I called the wood time, when I heated the place using just the logs I cut from the dead trees; but next week I'd have to get the oil tank filled to keep the temperatures up. Once the winter set in around here you could burn a whole forest and not catch up with the cold.

I walked outside across the clearing with the grave on my left and grabbed some logs. Each one fed the tang of the month it was stored into the luke-warm sun, and from the trees hundreds of rusty leaves fell scraping the bark on the way down, finding air again and floating, then landing with the sound of rain. Holding four logs in my arms I walked straight back to the door I'd left open, my eyes fixed to the ground. I didn't look but the damage was done—the fresh soil with the rock I put on top to keep predators away crept into the corner of my eye somehow, and my heart sank. By the time I was back in the cabin and stirring the fire, I missed him for the first time, missed him with a hammer strike against the heart, the awful moment when you know what gone really means. It means no one sees how you live, what you do.

And along with the sadness, something else crept in the door, a trace of something else, I mean. It must have come from the woodpile or ran in from the woods, because I'd not felt anything like it before.

6

WHEN I WAS VERY YOUNG MY FATHER TOLD ME THAT a man called William Shakespeare invented words, thousands of them, and to prove it he took out the plays of that man, *Julius Caesar, Cymbeline,* and *Richard II,* and showed me the small print at the bottom of each page where the words were written and what they meant. As part of my education he had me write out lists with Shakespeare's words in them, a few new words every day, using his fountain pen, and soon those words and the smell of ink entered my mind, and when I began to speak them in daily use my father was quietly pleased, smiling widely at me from behind his book, his socks drying by the fire. Thus every week I increased my vocabulary by twenty or so Elizabethan words, words come all the way from the 1500s to sit in my mouth and in my hand when I spelled them with their definitions. I remembered one day's set: *Blood-boltered* meant covered with blood, *besmoiled* meant covered with dirt.

I am a reader mostly, not a writer, but when I have to I can put some words together. Why then, so many years later at the age of fifty-one, I took a large sheet of paper and taped another to it and spread it on the floor in the last piece of sunlight left in the cabin and kneeled before it with a black marker, why I did that I don't know, and whatever I hoped to achieve was a distant and troublesome fleck on the horizon. But I found myself composing the first lines I'd written in a long time, apart from my signature or an address, writing in large capitals the words DOG SHOT and under it in smaller letters "On October 30 between the Wallagrass Lakes and McLean Mountain, Reward for Information," and under that my address at the post office where I collected my mail once a week, in winter sometimes every two or three weeks.

It is true that I composed these words by the stove fire when Hobbes was in the ground and beyond saving by letters, and I cannot say why I did it at all, though I think what crept in the door after me that same morning is what set me to writing, or else it was Shakespeare who inspired the poster. One of the two.

I warmed up the truck and drove with the announcement, reaching the good road along the St John River and travelled from there on to Fort Kent, where I set it on the wall outside the supermarket, taped it well to hold up against the wind and fastened it with a nail I banged in using a flat stone I brought in my pocket from the woods. It was early in the afternoon and I went inside to buy some groceries, bread and milk, some matches and vegetables, and then I stopped by the diner with a mind for black coffee and to sit in the heat and light and let my eyes see different things, hear different voices, for the cabin lay too heavy on my senses with Hobbes and everything. The woods were dark and wet, a mind of their own sometimes.

I set my gloves on the table and bowed my head slightly as the waitress stood at my shoulder with her notepad. She had seen me do this before and smiled.

She said, What would you like?

I stayed there for twenty minutes and enjoyed the cup and the way the steam heated my forehead until dark filtered along the streets and it was time to drive back. I said goodbye to her and passed the supermarket and glanced at the poster to see if it was still flat against the wall. I stopped and moved closer.

A large circle now surrounded the words Dog Shot and inside it in small letters, "Bye-bye dog" with exclamation marks after it, a punctuation mark my father had often complained about, a crutch for a weak word. I read on. Under that the person had written, "So what, one less dog. Get over it," and more exclamations. I stared at this for a minute in the street as people walked around me, giving me a lot of space, and then I took the poster down and rolled it up, placed it inside my coat.

I could not get back to the cabin fast enough, and then get inside the door fast enough, nor open the wood stove fast enough, nor stuff that poster inside it and burn it fast enough, watching the paper curl into an orange grip around the logs, thinking the cruelty of small towns was so sharp it might be a pencil and you could write with it, write on posters for lost and shot animals and mock them. My mind hopped around agitated on a high tree, would not come down, would not let me read, I tried—different books, different authors, warm and cold—no matter, an urgency wanted me out the door and walking, walking.

So I grabbed a coat and walked, out along the trail to the woods, to the place where I thought the shot came from when I heard it. Already a whole day gone by now but it felt like many weeks, and I replayed the sound to get my bearings. About five hundred yards along the edge of the trees, where it bordered a wide field, I saw a yellow shotgun shell in the grass and picked it up. It was a fresh cartridge, the metal untouched by rust, the yellow plastic still bright. And a few feet into the forest I found a pool of blood, and then drops of blood, frozen, heading toward the cabin.

This was the place. Hobbes had made it five hundred yards with a shotgun blast in him, shot from two feet away. I looked along the trail and saw the roof of the cabin where the trees dipped. Five hundred yards to get back to the cabin. I traced the ground, bending to and fro, looking for footprints but found none: the wind in the grass had erased them.

7

IT WAS LATE IN THE AFTERNOON. I HAD LET THE FIRE
go out.

I sat in the New England chair as the woods grew
quiet and hard and dark around the cabin and wondered what my father would have said to all of this,
what he would have thought of a grown man, his son,
all out of sorts over some lead and a dog, sitting by a
cold fire, if such a thing existed, sitting there in the dark
with something else that crept in the door and was
standing nearby, a feeling or tainted air that would not
be ignored but would not identify itself, moving from
room to room rustling furniture and drapes before
coming to the living room with its arms folded as if to
say, what now, now what. I sat in the chair as the room
light fell in sympathy with the woods, and I did nothing to win the room back, did not stir to read or make
some tea or listen to the shortwave radio. My father
would not have stood for it, he would have snapped his
book shut and told me to snap out of it. He had seen
too much fighting, and his father had seen too much

fighting before him. My blood was weaned off guns by two world wars.

Yet the yellow cartridge and the blood haunted me, a small action at the edge of a trail in a forsaken part of the world.

My father said that his father carried so many wars on his chest it was a wonder he could stand straight: medals from the Boer War, the First World War, and other small wars no one hears of anymore, skirmishes in the bush and such, scores or hundreds briefly dead and then wiped from history. He never fired a rifle after he came back from that war, and before he died, my grandfather gave his medals to my father and told him to keep them or to throw them away, he didn't care which.

I wonder why he would say such a thing, I said to my father one day, to which he said, World War One, and the Battle of the Somme, where your grandfather saw action, the lonely farmland in France where a million men fell to the ground: half a million British, two hundred thousand French, and over five hundred thousand Germans, shot or blown up by ordinance, where the Allies fired a week-long artillery bombardment of fifteen hundred guns and 1.6 million rounds before the opening assault and still lost fifty-eight thousand troops on the first day alone. How many people, Julius, do you think remember any of that?

Few people, maybe nobody, I said.

And that was barely eighty summers ago, he said. That's why your grandfather didn't care.

He took a deep-blue velvet box from the shelf and opened it, and there were the medals, heavier than I thought they should be.

But you kept them all the same, I said.

He nodded, the fire staining his spectacles, swallowed, and shut the box and went back to reading, and I left him alone for a while because he was a man who did not say much of what he felt.

He himself had fought in Holland in 1944 during the last desperate months of the Second World War when men claimed each building by the brick and fell in wet streets. At the end of it he threw away his carbine and came home, done with any kind of killing, and he never shot anything after that either.

I kept my grandfather's medals in the velvet box. You don't throw a million men away like that.

8

I GOT THE FIRE TO BURN HIGH ON SOME FRESH LOGS and sat before it with a mug of tea, watching the orange flames roar through the tempered glass. At such times, in the moments before I took up anything to read that is, silence sometimes took hold of me. Now that the hard weather had come, snow would follow and stay the winter. For some days past I heard the last of the Canada Geese cross the sky above the woods and fall in a deluge of cackles over the fields to rest on their way south to breeding grounds, stay silent for the night, hundreds of them on the plain, then rise with a thousand wings in the morning and circle until they drew an arrow in the sky under the sun, their compass south. This time of year stirred the restlessness in me too, perhaps because I saw how most creatures, when faced with a change in weather, either settle down or get out of town.

I had now lived fifty-one years in this cabin. In the summer months I worked some landscaping for the rich, mostly out-of-towners with holiday homes, and that suited me fine, since my business stayed my business, as those kinds of people don't generally want to be talking to anyone local. Along with that I did some machine work for an automobile shop fixing troublesome engines for the proprietor, a man who dangled at the end of an oily black rag and was glad to see me every spring, said I was a wonder with a machine, any machine on the face of the known world. I made enough from both jobs to sit out and survive the winter, and that was good, what you don't need isn't yours, my father said. But that was all I did, sit out the winter. I wondered if there was somewhere else in the world for me, and if I should have gone to the university, and what I would have done with my life if I did. I had never quite settled down or left and know I should have done more with my mind. If I were to write my life in one sentence up till now, I would say that at one point I lived in a cabin for fifty-one years.

9

ON WEDNESDAY I WOKE LATE WITH THE COVERS wrapped tightly around me all the way to my eyes, the way I slept. I had worn my long coat and socks to bed and fell asleep in them with the windows open for the fresh air. My breath rose in a fog of droplets as I gathered the courage to rise into the chill and boil some water for tea.

After some toast and butter I dressed in a sweater and my coat and a good pair of boots and walked to the barn. On the way I noticed that the orange and yellow nasturtiums had shriveled in their beds: the three nights in a row of even light frost had killed them. I could take away the plastic covering now, but all that for later. It was a very fine morning and some birds blew from one branch to another, swooping down for the seed I threw them and the hot water I put in the concrete fountain.

I shoved aside the door of the barn and made for the bench at the far end and unwrapped the rifle from the leather cover. I checked the bore, cleaned the chamber with solvent, and tested the trigger mechanism.

From a closet I retrieved a bag of .303 cartridges in 5-round clips and slipped one into the rifle before closing the door behind me, walking over again to the flowers to see if any were for saving, but they all drooped from their stems, long past rescue. I thanked them for their scent and for what they brought me by way of lifting my spirits all these months. I looked up: a snow flake or two drifted down out of a mostly blue sky, and the air in the clearing swam with the bark of trees in sunshine. I stood a moment at Hobbes's grave and did not know what to say or think. I would have given every book in the cabin, every penny I had to see him rise again from the hole. I would have forgotten the matter as best I could. But he did not rise, and so we now had come this far.

I set off for the woods with some bread in my pocket and hot tea in a small hip flask, and on a strap across my shoulder, the other thing my grandfather passed on to my father, a World War One Pattern 14 Lee-Enfield rifle.

10

I HIKED TO A SPOT A MILE AND A HALF INTO THE FOREST, walking in and out of the shade like a man in parts as the broken sun in the branches found me with little light and even less heat, and I walked slowly, for I was in no hurry, and even paused along the way to take a sip of the tea, wondering how anything in the world could feel warm in Maine, and how anyone could sneak up on any living thing in the late fall when the dry leaves cracked under boots so much. In summer these trees had formed a lush sanctuary from the heat; now most stood bare before the northern winds, sifting nothing.

I leaned between two trunks that formed a bench like a wishbone curling out over me, and rested the Enfield against my knee, ten pounds of wood and steel and resin pointing muzzle first into the sky, the only place you can safely point to no matter what's on your mind or finger.

I thought about the hour. Early on a fine morning. Any moment now.

I think I waited a long while, I'd say the best part of two hours, until a truck drove up, a big one with large antlers spreading from the middle of the front grille, humming slowly and quietly along the side of the forest about fifty yards off until stopping at the tree line. The man who got out looked in his early thirties, a big enough fellow wearing camouflage, his head shaven down bald on top, with long hair at the sides. That much I could tell and little more. He left the door open and changed his boots and then took a rifle from the back seat, shed the case, pointed it at the sky and then took out a bottle of beer and closed the door. Slinging the rifle on his shoulder, he walked forty paces to a tree where he climbed a ladder nailed into the trunk to reach a tree stand fifteen feet up, and there he leaned back and sipped from the bottle, his rifle—looked like a Winchester from where I sat—crooked across his lap, a fine rifle, no doubt. Now that he was a fixed distance from me, a matter of eighty yards, I could study him better. He was well-built, the type who can bring a fight to you and win easily, and his clothes appeared expensive and well-maintained. This was a careful and a patient man, confident that if patience and care went out of use, he could prevail with a more primitive manner of settling disputes. That was my reading of him, and so I elected to keep my distance.

He had probably decided to spend the morning here, waiting for the silence that brings deer in, a buck wandering at the edge of the field or bigger game down from the mountain. I brought the rifle up to my shoulder and fired from those eighty yards, one bullet that slapped into the folds of his neck. He grabbed at it as if for an insect and made a half-turn with eyes bigger than the forest, wondering what had happened. It was not a fatal shot, not yet, there was no spray of blood. I snapped the bolt back and chambered another round as he fell to the forest floor, his rifle tumbling after him to land flat on the leaves, bouncing once. That was good, the safety on his weapon was engaged. He groaned through the hole in his neck, it sounded. I moved from between the trunks and came up on him, the Enfield at a low angle and my finger off the trigger, because this man was done with shooting any thing for a long time.

He saw me coming and shook his head, kept shaking it as if saying no to a question I hadn't asked. I looked around the woods as I pulled out a drawing I had of Hobbes and bent to him.

Did you shoot this dog, I said.

He kept shaking his head.

Did you shoot this dog.

And then I said words I hadn't spoken for thirty years since learning them at my father's side. You are blood-boltered, I said. You are besmoiled.

I could see that he was a big man indeed, a slab of muscle two hundred and fifty pounds, with giant hands.

It was a fair while before I had managed to drag him all the way to the hollow two hundred yards off in the deeper forest, where I tipped him in, rolled him with my boot ahead of me until he was at the bottom. I lay his rifle on him and went back to the truck, driving it through the trees; it sailed easily through saplings, and when the truck and I rode into the grove of trees I wanted I jumped out. The truck continued into the dense brush and branches and on down a slope, and I followed it at a trot till it hit a tree, and I turned off the ignition and proceeded to cover it with more branches and leaves as best I could. I was on the way back to him when I remembered a magazine on the seat of the truck and went back to look: a publication called *Hunt*, with a huge elk on the front cover.

I went back to the man. I needed him farther down behind the boulder, so I jammed him tight into the small dry gully, just wide enough for him, well an inch too narrow, but my boot took care of that.

But you're heavy, I said and sighed, wiping the sweat off my head despite the cold. This was a tiring business, this dragging and driving. He could have knocked every sense out of my head if he'd made contact with that fist of his in close quarter fighting, made short work of me indeed. I was lucky as to the shot, that it brought him down and that it stopped him from getting up.

I think he said something before he went.

What? I think he said, and frowned, maybe from pain or at the words I spoke. There was no country, after all, of Elizabeth, and no country for Elizabethan words. I moved the page because his head moved to one side and stayed there. It was clear then that I would not be hearing from him on the matter.

I'm sorry, I said into the gully.

I walked to the cabin with *Hunt* in my inside coat pocket. The sun shone on the other side of me, and when I went to drink more tea from the flask I could shake but a few warm drops into my mouth.

I stood at the place where Hobbes always slept and looked at me with the flames in his eyes. His hairs were still stuck to the cushion. I missed my friend.

11

WITH OLD RIFLES YOU HAVE TO CLEAN THEM OR LOSE them, and the best time to clean them is when the powder is fresh in the barrel and before the fragments of the bullet jacket turn to a crust in the firing chamber. Whatever crud is in your bore can send your bullet off by a few inches, or worse, eventually backfire into your face if you're especially careless.

You clean it straight after.

I laid the rifle to rest on the bench in the barn and moved the rod with the brush through the bore to clear the powder from the grooves that made the bullet twist in flight, that gave it accuracy. Then I pinned a patch dipped in bore solvent to the rod polished off the residue in the barrel, then used a dry patch. That's it, it's that simple.

All that was left was to pour copper solvent mixed with some water into the chamber and wipe out the bullet fragments with a cloth. I wiped until the action shone, and I proceeded to walk the gun inside the cabin and hold it upside down over the stove to heat off the moisture, then brought the bore level to the window light and sighted along it for obvious obstructions: none. Rifle clean.

My father taught me to clean this rifle before I learned to shoot it. On any certain morning around the first of the month I could be sure I would hear him shout from his chair with his eyes lowered to his book, Julius, did you clean the Enfield?

I returned the rifle to the barn, as only a careless man leaves something like that, even unloaded, in a living room. And since I had placed another five rounds in the magazine I had no business storing it anywhere except in its case in the barn, having inserted the cartridges so that I would be able to fire at short notice. You don't want to be loading that thing under fire. People won't wait.

12

I COULD NOT CHOOSE A BOOK WITH THE RESTLESSNESS and wandered the shelves, in and out of the heat from the woodstove, walking along warm and cold books alike, they stood to attention with the life teeming in them. Then I remembered the list of Shakespeare words I copied out: they were on some pages shoved tight in between *Othello* and *Richard II*. I walked toward the spreading heat of the fire and pulled them, brought them to the New England chair and reviewed the list. There on the first page, in a young boy's careful writing, I saw my three words for one day: *Amort* meant dead, *Cullion* a base fellow, *Convoy* an escort.

I repeated them now, speaking low, as if afraid the words would take shape and walk off the page. And so many of them, pages and pages, hundreds of words.

I saw the shape in my coat draped on the wall hook and pulled out the hunting magazine and perused it after stoking the fire into an orange crackle. The pages felt glossy and expensive in my hands, large photographs and advertisements for weaponry, bows and

guns, boots and fatigues, Rifle Association badges, patri-
otic emblems, statistics on bullets, trajectories, different
load weights, error rates in flight. Enough statistics to
make you dizzy. A gentleman with gray hair kneeled
with his gun behind a bear splayed out on a mountain.
The caption: "Jake Larson harvested this very nice black
bear with a 12-gauge shotgun and the Federal saboted
slug load." Articles on the hunting life, another fellow
dangling two fat dead rabbits, big as two hands, at the
end of a string. Next page, a deer's head and a polished
black and gold shotgun leaning against a tree trunk,
with three shells fanning out from the butt: "I took this
big buck at seventy yards with the Winchester saboted
slug and the Browning Gold shotgun. The deer dropped
where it stood and did require a finishing shot." The
deer's eyes were open, the belly's fur matted around the
gunshot. A long essay on rifle choices for the beginner:
the centerfire rifle, the pump gun, the double barrel
(side-by-side or over-and-under), and the autoloader,
along with prices and makes, advantages and disadvan-
tages, types of game for each. And everywhere, photos
of men in baseball caps.

I studied the magazine in some detail, delaying at
the descriptions, losing myself in the riflery and the
camaraderie. A one-page announcement of the new
Remington slide action, 12-gauge model 870, Special
Field Edition. I read the phone numbers for the advertisements, the area codes, the small print and the poli-
cies, as I had been taught to read everything closely,

even the footnotes, for therein often lay the true tale. It was obvious: there was much that could be termed passion in these men's pursuits, a few women too. They loved their cold winter days in the field, the outing, the man and his gun in the wild, the open weather, the venture into danger. Good luck to them, I thought, for they gain excitement in the hunt, this much is obvious. And they were decked out in clothes and assisted by equipment that my grandfather or father never had going into the great battles that decided the fate of nations. I closed the magazine and slotted it between Victor Hugo's *The Retreat from Moscow* and *Les Miserables*, since my father had also instructed me never to throw away the written word.

13

At two-thirty in the afternoon on that same day I tired of sitting in the cabin, namely because the same restlessness came back to haunt my blood, my eyes, my hands, so much so that there was nowhere I could look where restlessness was not; and moreover the manner I had of breathing above ground when my friend and companion of late lay breathless under that same ground seemed unfair and brought his loss closer, made me seek another place to spend the hours. I therefore made my way to the barn, spread a handful of dripping seed for the birds that come night would be wanting for heat and food, and sure enough they came from all sides at once, seeing as I had the habit of doing this every day, and then I took the Enfield to the woods, walking the same trail that led me to the same place, singing a song from the great war I learned when a child: "It's a long way to Tipperary, it's a long way from home, it's a long way to Tipperary, to the sweetest girl I know." I sat by the same two crossed trees, saw a buck through the trees in the field.

14

My grandfather joined the war in progress, that is to say, he joined the war when the American army did, in 1917, hopped on a transport ship and crossed the Atlantic. And they gave him a good rifle, a Springfield .30 caliber. At the end of the war he made a trade with a British soldier, a man who had roamed the trenches with a Lee-Enfield for a year, picking off Germans with the Pattern 14 sniper version, chambered for .303 ammunition with a telescopic sight.

The last time my grandfather killed a man was in the Second Battle of the Marne when he fired at German troops crossing the river. They took heavy losses, and after that, as my father explained, my grandfather never seemed to be able to hit his targets, firing wide or too high, and he proceeded to miss his way through to the end of the war. On the last day of fighting, November 11, 1918, he sat with his friends counting down the minutes to the Armistice at eleven o'clock. A British soldier left his position and

approached the German lines on a reconnaissance mission. His friends called him back. The Germans waved him back, told him to wait. He did not. The Germans shot him. The war ended sixty seconds later. Everyone got out and shook hands. My grandfather traded the rifle that had lately been off target so often for the British sniper's Enfield, called it an exchange of blood, remarking that the sniper said he had twenty-eight kills with the Enfield in almost two years.

So it came to pass that my grandfather arrived back in Maine early in 1919 carrying a rifle he never shot that had killed twenty-eight men, and though he kept it in good condition, he never shot it at any time after the war either, because he had seen enough of that, and smelled enough cordite, he said, and the war had bred all the gunnery out of him. And when he died and my own father officially owned the rifle, he in turn never fired it, only taking it from the wooden case for cleaning every few months.

When I was twelve he brought me out to the barn and took the rifle from its wooden case and leather wrap, brought me with him into the woods and taught me how to use it. On that day I became the first to shoot that rifle since 1918, and I had a hard time even lifting it straight, it weighed almost a pound for every year of my life. My father told me that the rifle I was holding had certainly ended the life of a number of German soldiers in the trenches, most of those officers whose wives and children received letters in small

German towns and villages in the weeks that followed, letters that expressed official regret. When he told me this, the rifle seemed to get even heavier. He said that I was qualified to use the rifle when I felt mostly comfortable with a little fear mixed in. And never forget, he said, to fire from the shoulder and breathe as you pull the trigger.

Standing in the woods with him and the rifle, barely holding it up straight, I felt mostly fear. I looked down the sights and instead of the bright woods of Maine saw the shadows of gray battle dress six hundred yards away across a mud-drenched battlefield, ghosts of men long dead still hovering in the sights. At that point the rifle was at its heaviest. I smelled powder, I thought, but my father said that the powder was long gone, the bore and action well cleaned.

He laughed as I faltered and told me that a gun held nothing more than bullets; it took a man to hold the gun, an eye to train it on a target, and a finger to pull the trigger and set the bullet in flight. He said a gun will shoot a tin can or a president and was no more good or bad than the people who used it.

15

I SAT WAITING IN THE WOODS AND IGNORED THE BUCK in the field. Some time passed, not much. The man who eventually came into view moved as though from out of the trees themselves, so quietly did he walk. I saw nothing, but I heard him. I lifted my eyes only and did not stir another muscle in any part of me, and even then the seconds went by and he was still invisible, and I thought he was a part of my mind coming toward me and not in the woods. In the end, the boots gave him away: he was wearing new or recently polished boots, I heard the tiny squeak, and then I saw him, dressed in fatigues, camouflaged well against the dark brown and green undergrowth, carrying his gun in both hands, angled upward and ready for a quick shot, his index finger laid across the trigger housing like a soldier trained in warfare. This was a man who liked to stalk his prey, to walk with it, shadow it, strike in a moment like a thunderbolt. I surmised his weapon to be therefore loaded, and it looked like a slug gun, lethal up to a hundred yards, a wound mortal for sure. He was moving at ninety yards from me I gauged, and he seemed taken with the big buck now feeding in the open field, and he stared at it, head down, and lifted and brought down each leg with silence and cunning, a feat for a big man wide at the shoulders and with a neck used to carrying for a living, a construction man from appearances. Red stubble uniform on his skull. He should have been wearing an orange vest: that was careless of him.

He lifted his shotgun in the brush and aimed, and that is when I darted from the two trees and swung the rifle to my shoulder, and breathed halfway out and squeezed the trigger. He dropped where he stood, like the forest falling down in his clothes. The buck was already half way across the field, covering yards a step, head first to the horizon, as if shot from the same gun.

He could not have known his luck as he ran, that deer.

I approached the man who had pitched forward onto his face and was breathing heavily, snorting against leaves and such. The bullet had found him between the shoulder blades and a foot down from the neck, and he reached for it as did the other man that morning, and to no account. There was no pulling the lead out, no undoing the havoc it spread among any soft organs going in.

What came next? I did not feel the rush of air. I only believe I did, and that is very much a different thing.

It was a knife on my neck but no knife when I turned and swung the rifle to my left as I heard the thunk in a tree trunk behind me. Well, well. The second of an unusual pair of hunters, wherever he was. And this one carrying a crossbow and walking parallel to his friend somewhere on the other side of the woods: he had heard and seen the shot and knew what was what and let loose upon me. I was cut at skin level. This man, however, would not make the same mistake twice and was no doubt already inserting another bolt in his weapon, strong enough to go through me if he found the mark. I brought the rifle up to my shoulder and grasped the bolt handle, dragging it back and forward to eject one round and chamber the next, hoping that the sight of a rifle pointed in his direction would get the man to stir. Move! Move! Anything to make him move.

What he did was not to move but breathe, and I saw the wisp of breath, targeted it, and fired.

My hand was straight away on the bolt right above the trigger and moving another round into the chamber. First came the groan, and again I saw the forest move, as this one, also in fatigues, went soft in the knees and went down on them. I walked to him then, seeing as he did not appear to have suffered a fatal wound. When I reached him he was attempting to reload as blood pumped from his right shoulder, spreading red in the fibers of the cloth.

He watched me approach, slack-jawed, eyes

drooping in some degree of pain, I could tell. They swung lazy and insouciant to his friend.

You were unlucky in the shot, I said. That was a good shot. You had me almost, but you aimed for the thinnest part of me.

He fumbled with the bow and I kicked it away from the tangle of his hands. There was not much meat on this one, bony enough, though he had a wiry texture to his strength no doubt, and liable to chill easily around the joints. He developed a shake about the limbs, the shock that was, and shock is worse than any wound.

Amort, bow hunter.

You son of a bitch, he said.

No need for that, I said, and shot him back into the ground, smelled the cordite out of the second hole in him like a black flower.

I walked to the first one who had gone down and not moved since but was praying heavily or saying some fashion of words directed not at me nor himself, but at another not present with us. I slid another round into the chamber and placed the Enfield on the ground and withdrew the drawing of Hobbes from my shirt pocket, turning the man around on his back, holding the drawing to his face, observing his features directly for a reaction.

Are you the shooter of my dog, this dog?

He was saying something, but the shock took the saliva from his mouth and with it the chance to manufacture a word to say to me. Still he tried. His mouth moved in the dirt as if he were talking to the earth and not to me at all. His right eye was wet, the snot grew under his nose, I saw some purple at his kidney where the jacket was pulled up. There went his jaw again, opening and closing into the dirt, saying his secret words. Keep them to yourself, that is fine, they won't change anything.

But he was gone already, gone from shock, he shook his head or his head shook him, and I asked him again, asked him in truth did he shoot my dog, was he a shooter of dogs, and he sank at the neck into the leaves, and when I bent to lift him up, he was a damp red rag of a man dressed in camouflage.

I said, You fired from hiding, but I saw you. And your convoy is a cullion.

I thought I observed a spark in him, a puzzlement.

Prithee, I said then, was your hiding not hidden enough? I took you, harvested you.

I waited by him while he left and said an Ave into his ear, though he was well past hearing. With everything that had happened, the man who shot my dog was most likely dead by now, I thought, and plenty who would say what I did was wrong. And they would be right, because two out of the three were not the shooter, and those two I had killed unjustly, no question of that, especially since I was of sound mind and an otherwise principled man.

All that remained was to clean up the forest, which entailed bringing the pair to their resting place. After a bit of thought I dragged them to the earlier man's truck and placed them inside, across the bench seat, one on the other, head to toe for balance. They were friends, after all. After the leaves and branches were piled above the windshield, I was on the trail back to the cabin in no time, where I cleaned the rifle and laid it in its case in the barn.

16

A WOMAN ONCE SAID I SHOULD GET A DOG FOR COMpany if not for hunting. She said that a man should not live alone as I did, in the woods. And we passed over lists of all God's creatures that might keep me company and we settled on a dog, a good choice given where and how I lived.

That was four years ago.

We drove to the dog pound in Fort Kent because I wasn't going to buy a dog and not a fancy one either, they take up your time and are better off in large houses and the like. When we got to the pound we walked the line of cages, the rows of paws and heads aching for a run somewhere, a bit of fresh air, barking for masters who had let them go in all manner of ways, lost them, let them out of cars at supermarkets and driven off, beat them away with sticks or starved them. And they were waiting for those masters to come back and find them, you could see them searching every face for a face they knew.

Here, she said, and we stopped at a cage where a dog the size of my hand was pacing in a circle.

The boy who worked there nodded sadly as if he knew this fellow's time was soon up; the breed and his size would win no one's heart or a home to him. He would be put to sleep.

The boy said, He was brought in by a couple who had baby twins and couldn't have him around the house, they were afraid. We've had him a week already.

Can you take him out a second, I said.

The boy opened the cage and hauled the brindle-colored fellow out by the neck, mostly terrier but with some pit bull about the mouth and chest. I held and bent to him, and didn't the little bastard nip me in the nose.

I'll take that one, I said, pointing to him, even though he was the only one out of his cage, the only one in my hand. That's how definite I was. We took him back home that same day. He got out of the truck and ran around the clearing, stretching his legs, busy taking possession of the place, figuring what he owned, all the space he had suddenly and out of nowhere.

It is true that was a happy time for me, not then so much because of the dog as the woman who asked me to find one for myself. One day a few weeks before that, she had walked out of the woods and across the clearing around the cabin, and when I came out to greet her, she told me she got lost when out for a walk on a late spring day, that her car was parked a ways off somewhere, and she said it without a trace of fear. To walk in these woods meant she was local. She pointed to the flowers, now just appearing.

You grow flowers.

I nodded. That I do. They keep me company out here.

She seemed to like that response and looked down at her hands, which she had taken from her gloves. They were white and perfumed with a cream I could smell from where I stood, a light ointment most likely. I asked her if she would like a cup of tea.

When she saw the books she opened her mouth but said nothing.

I fiddled with the kettle, letting the water run from the tap till it was good water, eyeing the chair for papers or a book I might have left on it. The fire was hot and splintering pleasantly but the woman ignored it and passed along the shelves in trails of sunlight curled by trees and the window frame. Her fine shoes clicked on the bare floorboards.

But there must be thousands, she finally said. Those words took a while coming out of her. Her accent had a trace of the local about it.

Three thousand, two hundred and eighty-two, I said.

I've never seen anything like this, and she smiled and clapped her hands. And you have green plants everywhere too, and those paintings. This is wonderful.

She ran her finger along the spines of the books,

feeling the imprint of the title letters. She leaned close and smelled the leather, closing her eyes. I lost sight of her when she moved beyond the H books but heard her murmur as I carried the tea out of the kitchen and found her sitting on the chair, smoothing the spider plant, the only one that could go that close to the fire.

You sit well in that chair, I said.

That was the first day I met Claire. She came back the day after, and some weeks later she came again, and this time the night fell in the middle of a talk and she stayed until the morning, slept beside me in the bed, and soon enough my arm was around her and she did not move away, so we grew warm together and slept, and before we did she asked me to take off my coat, that I had company. I felt her giggle beside me.

She said I was like a straw man, a blond scarecrow with blue eyes, my feet sticking over the end of the mattress. And so tall, she said, you are seen for miles with that pale face, the whitest face and blue eyes and blond hair.

Yes, from head to toe she measured me at six foot three, which was news to me as I had never thought too much about it, and had long since bowed my head without thinking in most doorways, though I did not cross that many except for my own. She told me I was the handsomest man she ever saw, and that was a strange thing to hear from a woman who could have been with any man, but she chose me, this lady who came out of the woods in her coat. I was happy, felt an ease that had not been mine since the days of my father. I lay beside her and thought again of what lay around me in the darkness: a life simple, the mattress on boxes, the chair with a red velvet cushion that my father used to read Shakespeare from, yes, the best piece of furniture in the house, and fine Rosenthal china for the tea, two cups and two saucers. I had much to be grateful for.

She asked me if I missed my father and mother.

Dead a long time ago now, I said, and that's the truth.

She asked me what happened, and I told her that my mother died as I passed through her body into my own breathing. She was a person I killed by being born, I said.

You didn't kill her, Claire said. And she's not dead, not in your mind she said, and touched my forehead. I flinched, not used to touching.

I liked her more for saying that. But the truth was that I did kill my own mother, the first person I ever killed, and no words can counter that. I missed seeing her alive by a minute. I often spoke to my mother at night and whispered to her, hoping that somewhere a trace of her could hear me, a touch she left on a candlestick, a breath stuck to the window glass she looked out of one morning.

If love leaves an echo, I said, she is with me still. If not, I have nothing of her.

★ ★ ★

The summer sun moved the days longer and longer apart, and soon the flowers filled the view in the window with yellow and deep reds and purples. Butterflies swam along the fat grass and up into the stems, drawing their own greens and browns through the mornings. Claire came and went from her home in St. Agatha, a small French town on Long Lake, almost twenty miles east of me, where she lived near her parents. I asked her why a woman like her, in her late thirties, had not married, and I added that late thirties was still very young in a woman, because I knew the delicacy of such matters from all the books. She said that she had once had a fiancé but that it had not lasted. She watched me closely as she said this. I didn't know why I was being inspected so closely, and I nodded.

These things happen, I said. People come together, people part.

She seemed to relax then, took a deep breath and added, And I think I will have a child one day.

I saw a daughter in her eyes, I don't know why.

She will be happy, I said.

She held my hand then and nodded. You are a gentle man, Julius Winsome. Then she laughed and said, Some weeks ago I went for a walk in the woods and I found a very gaunt giant living in a tiny cabin.

We called the dog Hobbes, from a philosopher, the first name we found when we pulled a book at random from the shelf; so the luck of a draw got Hobbes his name. It might easily have been Charles or Hugo or Stevenson or Leviathan, thankfully not the latter, with all the syllables. One Wednesday evening she brought me a dog's nest from a shop in the town and Hobbes took to it warmly, spent many happy days curled up in it, taking more space as the weeks passed and he grew to the edges. Terriers are smart. He quickly learned the words "Walk," "Run," and "Ride," the three words he knew, or at least the three he let me know he knew. The sound of the truck keys also brought him bounding from the woods or scratching to get out the door. With his head out the window and a breeze in his face as we drove along the countryside, he was a dog run through with happiness, for they lead short lives and have an extra sense for each passing moment. They eat with all their hearts, they play with all their hearts, they sleep with all their hearts.

And whenever Claire visited, he heard the sound of her truck before I did and ran between her legs and jumped up to lick her face.

That's why he licks you, to put his scent on you, I said.

She said, And I thought he liked me.

That too, I said.

17

In the second month of summer Claire was arriving twice a week, sometimes when I was working the gardens of the rich around Fort Kent or at the machine shop. I never locked the door because I had Hobbes, who had grown into a friendly but punchy little pit-bull terrier, so she let herself in and read the books or, she said, sat on the porch and watched the woods or tended to the flowers. I had no telephone or television, and I think she liked the silence that the woods sheltered, even if the guinea hens cackled, and she grew fond of the rhythm that soothed away the worry she seemed to carry with her, an anxiety that came from nowhere and had nowhere to go. In the evenings we drank some tea and wine she brought from the supermarket in paper cups and I sometimes fished out the Turkish cigarettes I kept for special occasions. What I loved was the anticipation on the drive home of being with her, seeing her in the evenings, her smell, her touch that made me shiver alive like a plant, the joy when I saw her truck parked in the clearing.

One day toward the end of summer, she didn't come any more. I was just getting used to her and didn't understand why she stayed away. I heard nothing for months and wondered if something had happened, so I drove to Fort Kent and looked for her. This was difficult because she never once brought me to her parents, who she said lived in St. Agatha, nor to her home or her friends. I let it go because people have their reasons and if you have to ask you already have asked one question too many. I was sure her parents were fine people who didn't know about me or did and didn't want anything to do with me. Anyway I finally bumped into her outside a small cafe.

She looked sad and said, He has a house and a business.

Who, I said.

You know.

No, I don't. I had no idea what she was referring to, though it sounded like another man.

She read my mind or my features because she said that she had been with him for some time. He lived in the town too. Maybe I was supposed to know.

I have to look after myself too, she said.

I said, Yes, that's the truth, and I lost her in that second. I did not know who the other fellow was, and it felt to me as if she had indeed been seeing him all the while. And she was gone from me.

All of this was years ago, but even now I keep an eye on the woods, sometimes the white woods, sometimes the green woods, hoping some evening she will walk out of them and back to me, and then I see that I'm only dreaming and would in any case not be able to welcome her again. She chose her life and everything in it, every stitch. Perhaps things don't happen for a reason, they happen because people do them.

After she told me the news, going back to being on my own was hard, and winter soon came and hardened it more.

18

AFTER RETURNING TO THE CABIN FROM THE INCIDENTS which had occurred in the woods earlier in the day—I mean the meeting with the two men and how they came to be resting on one another—I ate some dinner and then read Shakespeare, his word-inventions.

When I was young my father checked the list of Elizabethan words often, making sure that I learned at least three a day. Going down the column I could see that on a certain Tuesday—I could see from the entry—on a Tuesday when I was nineteen I learned five C words, so it must have been raining outside or I may have neglected to learn any the previous day. I checked the list: *cinque-pace* was a dance, *colour* meant pretense, *churl* was a rude person, *coil* turmoil, and *cog* cheat. I sipped the tea and leaned back on the red cushion, enjoying the moment enough to make up sentences: "He did a cinque-pace when I shot him, the churl. The second one meant to kill me, but I cogged him of that chance by killing him."

I said more sentences because the day felt long to

me, and repeating them brought me back to when life was simpler, no unpleasantness or confrontations. I would have shown them to my father had he been standing at my shoulder or sitting by the fire himself, puffing tobacco in his pipe. But with life's events one must win one's own approval. There is no one to show anything to, no one who will say well done.

All the following day, a sunny, cold Thursday, the kind of day favored by hunters, I remained home and listened to the shooting from far off, starting early when I was not long out of bed and making the fire and the first pot of tea, and continuing well into the afternoon as I gathered more books to the chair to read, the shots thinner and weaker because the hunters were far off. I looked out and saw Hobbes' grave, the last of the color on the dead stalks hanging on. There was little that was beautiful about the world, I thought, and little that the world of men brings to it at the best of times. What there was, he brought to me.

The pink petals hung raw and shook with the cold and wind. How they hung on out of season, the struggle of it, the strength it took. Not long now, and they'd be brown stains on a stalk.

Before I went to bed, I did some more writing. The fire was low and I had to squint, and on top of that I wasn't much of a writer indeed, but this was a time for committing words.

19

IT CAME TO PASS THAT ON THE THIRD DAY AFTER HOBBES'S shooting I drove into Fort Kent with a new poster spread on the seat beside me, drove cautiously late that afternoon along the dirt road, swerving slowly around the same potholes that I bumped over in my desperate drive with Hobbes. There was no hurry now, and I didn't pick up speed until the trees to each side petered out and the sky and its clouds opened up above the paved road to the town, but as I rounded the bend at the outskirts I came onto a checkpoint, slowed down, then stopped. A policeman asked me my name and had I seen any men up my way, that some were missing. He seemed to know where I was from, because he mentioned the general area where I lived in passing, and his eyes darted around the truck while I said no, that I hadn't seen any such men. He thanked me and waved me on, and once in the town proper I parked in my usual place behind the supermarket. Taking the new poster, I carried it to the front of the store and hammered it into the timber notice board with a hammer and nail from the barn and standing back to read the words: DOG SHOT. October 30. Reward for information. J. Winsome, Post Office Box 271.

It was the best thing to do, because someone saw the first poster, if only the person who wrote all over it; otherwise I might have to explain one day why the first poster went up and came down the same day around the time that various incidents were alleged to have occurred, and if taking down the poster meant I knew something no one else knew, or words to that effect, whatever way lawyers talk when there's trouble. The pity was that I no longer needed information, and if anyone had some they could hold onto it for the rest of their lives for all I cared. The second poster could rot. But let's see who turns up.

After buying matches, milk, tea, bread and butter, and putting them in the truck, I walked across the street and down two blocks to the diner. Sure enough, I noticed the wind stiffening, the rain harder when it fell in fitful drops, as if they held snow inside them for ballast. I was glad then of the warm blast of air as I opened the door of the diner, and of the bright lights, and of the few people who sat huddled over soup and hot beverages. The waitress was different but brought the same make of coffee to the same table I liked and said the same word, Enjoy.

At another table, two men in lumberjack gear bent to their drinks, discussing a missing man.

He went hunting two days ago, no sign of him.

Where did he go?

We're not sure, I heard his wife said west in the valley, maybe as far as Allagash, to the mountain woods, but Jack could have veered north on a whim and even gone across the border.

Or down to Moosehead Lake, the other said.

The first said, It's got the sheriff spooked, since there's word of another couple of men from Frenchville way missing, though they were out for a week and are late only a day or two. Still, there's a coincidence.

I kept an ear to what they said, kept my eyes down, finished my coffee and left some change, tipped my cap to the waitress and left. So, three men missing, one of them called Jack. Sounded like a decent man. The word had spread fast for some men gone off to the woods with guns. They must have been more local than I thought, men from the area, with families, with times they were due back home. I was sorry to hear a wife being mentioned. But that was to have been expected at some stage. You can't get away from that once the numbers go up.

There were lights strung above the street at the other end of town, a festival organized by the town library where children dressed as scarecrows, and the banner announced a barn dance and book sale to be held this Sunday. On the small green, a tall spreading pine tree lit the falling night. Good to have something that brought a glow to the streets up here where the dusk was so early: window candles, silver stars and such on trees, children's eyes filled with new hours of light, what this festival promised them even in winter's longest dark.

As I walked back to the supermarket I saw Claire across the road at the same time as she saw me. She raised her hand in half a wave and I stopped, then she looked each way and crossed the road, and I waited outside the window of an electronics shop in the gusty wind while my insides shook. I wrapped the long coat around me to stop it flapping.

Looks like weather coming, she said, stepping to the curb.

Yes, I said. That it does.

The store window had about twenty televisions on all the shelves, it seemed to me, and each one had a different channel showing, flashing images of bodies behind me in the corner of my eye, people dancing, singing, talking, with holiday lights already draped on the televisions, flashing too, with signs saying that there were only seven short weeks to Christmas. Even though the sound was turned down they did all the talking for us, because we said nothing to each other for a while as people walked by. A flurry of white swept the street and was gone like a lighthouse beam.

I didn't want to be staring at her, so I gave a quick glance. Her hair was different, more curly. It was better when it was straight, suited her bone structure that way. After some time passed with us standing there she said,

Julius, I'm so sorry.

For what then?

For everything. She kissed me all of a sudden and said, Be careful.

Of what then?

I don't know. I often think of you alone up there. Just a feeling.

Another gust blew the lights sideways on the tree, a colder wind, bringing snow for sure. I wondered about that comment of hers. Then we both said nothing again for some seconds. I'm not good at saying goodbye, especially if it's forever. I don't know, I felt a frozen wind blow around her as if encasing her in stone, or maybe it was just going around her and heading straight for me.

How's Hobbes? she said

He's fine.

What was the point in making her sad? Sharing my own sadness would not make it less, only double it.

You know I love that dog.

I know. He's fine.

A man joined us, he was dressed in a constable's uniform, and he slotted himself at her side without looking at me.

Hi, Honey.

He kissed her and hugged her close to him. I watched something above her head that wasn't there just to put my eyes somewhere. She smiled and nestled her head on his shoulder. He smooched her hair, stroked it. The television danced behind me, the boxes this time, not the people in them. They were yelling at me to go home and be away from this town.

Let's go, he said to her. It's getting late. Remember we've got friends coming over for drinks.

He still didn't look at me.

Troy, this is Julius, she said.

He turned his head and stared, empty, mouth hard, gave a nod only a marksman could have observed. I held out my hand but he was already sheparding her away.

I heard him say after only a few steps, Don't tell me that's the guy.

Shhh, she said.

You went out with *him*? What were you thinking?

Shut up, will you, Troy? He's got good hearing.

He said something else while they crossed the road, I could tell by his lips and the waving he was doing.

I continued on, a short walk the rest of the way to the supermarket. People tumbling out with shopping in the rush hour, cars dusted with flakes pulling up and flashing people who waited with groceries on the pavement outside. I glanced at the poster to make sure it was still there. Yes, and not only that, someone had written across it in a heavy pen, "People are more important than dogs!!! Feed the people this Christmas!!" I ripped it off the wall and a couple moved aside to give me room as I tore it into strips and stuffed the shreds into my coat pocket. Fine, I'm done with posters now. No more writing.

I drove home under the festival lights of Fort Kent and on into the night where there were no lights but the stars, and none were out that evening, or they were but strung out over low cloud, the type of cloud that races across the skyline at twilight, races with the smells of the earth and of the air, pushing the air in front of it, cold air.

Night fell as I cut through the countryside. When the headlights scoured out the dirt lane to the cabin I thought I saw Hobbes run up to them, as he was always doing, running out of the night and across the lights, sniffing the bags after I brought them into the kitchen and put them on the floor, looking for his treat.

Now, driving in the dark, I summoned my boyhood friend Shakespeare and tried another sentence: "My stomach was in a coil when that man hugged Claire. He had some color about his face, the way he ignored me."

After she left me I had gotten to love that dog. He always greeted me when I returned home. For the rest of that summer he ran from his spot in the hot woodpile, from his walks in the woods, where he went for solitude or whatever drives them there, ran to see me after my landscaping work, ran to greet me when I was happy, ran to greet me when I was unhappy, ran to greet me when I was distracted, vague, thoughtful. When my hands gripped the steering wheel or lay loose as the truck rumbled up the dirt road, lurching with shovels and picks or unencumbered, he ran to greet me. Dogs know only loyalty and find their own lives inside it.

And they know when you're not right, they'll sniff the disease in you, the low light in your blood, and put their mouths there, be it your kidney or your arm—and they'll stick by you until you're okay. Find me a human who'll do that. They bark a certain way and it means certain things: you have to hear the tones and the length and how he places his head and what his tail is doing. They don't have words so they use their whole bodies to make words. Sound and head angle and tail and what not. They talk with their whole body. People use their bodies not to talk, hands in front of mouths, turning sideways, never listening. They put fear in their dogs. You want to know the man, look at his dog.

And when I thought he was running up to me, I thought a miracle was mine, some strangeness in the woods had produced him back, my Hobbes, the terrier, an early Christmas gift for Julius Winsome. I would have a fire on in no time, find a treat or drive him to Fort Kent with the heater on and the window open so he could stick his head out and still be warm. That would be just the start.

But when I parked the truck with the lights shining on the flowerbeds, the grave was undisturbed.

20

THURSDAY NIGHT THE SNOW FELL.

The wind stopped and the temperature went up slightly, I could tell from the drafts and the silent sweep of powder that shook itself across the fields, the woods, the cabin roof, and across and along the rest of Maine it seemed. But for the trees the wind would strike the cabin directly.

There is a day, an hour when winter comes, the second it slips in the door with its weather and says, I am here. If snow falls early enough, it drifts down into red forests and piles along lakes ringed with blue ice, but the visit is temporary: the white handprint of north vanishes with the next sunny day, polished off the hills and trees of Maine by the cloth of sunshine, the blow of warm fall breath on wood. If late, winter arrives on the back of a windstorm that blows every color before it but white, while under it, lakes turn to frozen spit and bare trees split, cracked open, and the forests stretch up to the shivering lit skin of the northern lights.

Maine, the white star that burns from November, it rules a cold corner of sky. Here, only short sentences and long thoughts can survive: unless you're made of north and given to long spells alone, don't trespass here from then. Distances collapse, time is thrown out. Children skate their names on ponds, sleds drag dogs in front of them. People defeat the winter by reading out the nights, spinning pages a hundred times faster than a day turns, small cogs revolving a larger one through all those months. The winter is fifty books long and fixes you to silence like a pinned insect; your sentences fold themselves into single words, the hand of twelve makes one hand of time. Every glance ends in snow. Every footstep sinks North. That's time in Maine, the white of time.

It is also the time when an entire day squeezes in through the single bedroom window, and I stayed in bed most of the day, the blankets warmer than the air.

But I had things to do first. I ran to the woodpile and hauled in some logs before they got damp, and I covered the rest with green tarpaulin, folded once. After a meal of potatoes and fried fish I went out again with the flashlight and walked the flowerbeds and said good-bye to the last shades of pink and red, since by morning they would be cast under white, and soon covered. I hoped that the long snow of winter, now just begun, would keep my friend warm. I leaned to the ground and sank my fingers into the snowfall above where he lay.

I stood in the clearing as it whitened and looked up into the broken pieces of the night around the flakes.

Winter.

PART TWO

Night of November 2nd

21

THAT NIGHT IT WAS AS IF THE WIND SIMPLY BLEW through the house and blankets, as if nothing blocked the weather from my body. I lay in bed, waiting for a strain of heat to measure me and fit me into sleep. I heard noises, surely the crackling chill in the timbers of the cabin. Unless: wait, was that Hobbes at the door scratching? Had he somehow woken up and clawed his way out of the flower beds? I had heard of such things in history books, people in coffins waking up, wood found in their fingernails. That, or there were men about in the dark. If so, no matter: before lying down I brought the Enfield into the bedroom and leaned it against the wall.

I rose, let the cover fall away to the coat, and made for the door with the rifle loose in one hand, but when I opened it, one knife flew at my face, my hands, my feet, three instant cold blades from the wind. I shielded my eyes to no avail: no dog anywhere in sight, no paws and a head waiting to come in. I lingered to be sure, stood there for a minute before going back inside and pulling on the wool socks and a sweater under the coat. The wind must have infected me now, I shook that hard. I dressed myself fully by the bed. To fall asleep and be defenseless, to lie still while the forest swarmed around, that could not be. Better covered now, I was off again, this time all the way outside, to the grave.

Bending close I saw nothing that showed Hobbes had freed himself. I traced no evidence of even weak marks, the softening tracks of a running dog. So the howl and scratch at the door was only the cold after all. I stood at the forest edge wrapped in the coat and looked back at the cabin: the weak light of the frigid bedroom I had just left glimmered in the cracks of the side window, otherwise all was black, open to the elements but for a few inches of timber and a lining of books.

I waited for nothing. And nothing arrived. A deep ice stole its way into my heart. I felt it settle in and numb the valves and quiet the wind that blew inside my frame, heard it set upon my bones and breathe silence into the brittle spaces, everything that was broken. At that moment my heart knew the peace of cold. I gave up on my friend, and the night watch was done, for only his spirit would ever come to me again.

22

IF THE NOISE WAS NOT FROM THE GRAVE, THE UNEASE was elsewhere, and I could not stay out here standing sentry for that long. The suspicion that drew me out was perhaps all that could be called grave tonight: what had stayed at the back of my mind, a worry like wings.

I did not want to suspect Claire of anything, and did not, until I remembered our recent conversation on the street when she seemed to sense that all was not well with me. How would she know? Was her hand in this? Perhaps she belonged so completely now to another man that she decided to remove anything from that summer that still attached itself to me, and all that was left was Hobbes.

Such a thought, that Claire brought a gun out along the trails to my cabin and ended the life of the dog she helped rescue. It was well beyond my means to harm her, or any woman—and in that event my father would never have tolerated such a thing—but the thoughts would not disperse from my mind. Had she killed him?

Though the cold was something fierce, I hugged the coat about me more and leaned into the sheltered side of a tree trunk.

23

TO LOOK FOR EVIDENCE MEANT SHARPENING THE
details of what was already known, re-seeing what was
already seen. And it slowly came to me, what was both-
ering me, some evidence of a trick she played with others to bring this dog into my life and then take him
away. I resolved however to think things over before
anything else was done.

The first evidence of guilt was the way she turned
up at the cabin that day in early summer. She walked
past the flowers that stained the grass blue and yellow
under the Maine sky, wide and shallow and ice blue. I
was in the kitchen reading, and the wind blew from the
south through the open window and through all the
rooms, seeking out the last smells and shadows of
spring, and the new summer grazed my skin with a
warm whisper, its first word. I rose from the armchair
when I heard her: my face had been buried in a book
and now it filled the glass as I watched.

Some hens ran after each other in the sunlight under the smell of burning pine and past the truck. I stepped out onto the porch under smoke that swept down from the chimney.

She said, I was in the area. I don't know, I got lost I think.

It made perfect sense to me then, as if she had just raised her wrist with a watch on it and told me the time of day in the middle of the street back in the town.

If that's so, I said, why don't you come in then and have some of the tea.

To her the walls must have looked like they were made out of books, leather that stretched along the eye. I walked behind her to the sink and watched the house fit around her as she stood under the door frame that separated the large first room from the second. She glanced at the oak floor and the wood stove, watched the fountain outside the small side window: a bird wriggled through the water. She whispered how few of the paintings had people in them, the ones on the walls hung by my father and grandfather, one a brown landscape of bare trees, others of seashores, gardens, haystacks, climbing above the bookshelves.

I went off to play a record, some piano music. I should have pressed my question at once about this sudden visit. Outside it fell down some short rain, the flowers dripped, and the notes dripped from the bedroom, a tune by Satie from my father's days. I poured the boiling water onto the tea bags and handed her a mug with a spoon.

You haven't changed much, she said.

I said, I don't think we've met.

No, it's my sister. She was a few classes behind you in school when you went there. She described you.

Though it made little sense, it was what she said. When the shower ended the sun shone through the wet glass and warmed the red roofs in one of the paintings. I wondered why she got lost here and not somewhere else but did not want to ask, since people usually choose the place they get lost in and she must have had her reasons. Anyway I had much of the rest of the day free, and all that was left was to run into the town and pick up carrots and fish and some bread.

Was I rude to just turn up like this, she said.

I asked her what other way there was to turn up.

Her car was in the woods, she said, a half mile away where the road was still wide enough: she wanted to go for a long walk today and kept going. She had to go home now. That must have been her first mission, to see the cabin, to count how many lived here, a short count as it turned out.

I told her I would bring her back as this was no place for walking in once evening made its way through the trees, even in summer. The odd large creature made its way across the river from Canada and might not take well to the surprise. We made our way under the leaves, mostly in silence along a brown line that wound itself into the undergrowth. The way was narrow enough to tell me that the last part of the journey had been too close for her to drive: the branches touched each other across it. In the truck it was just a matter of keeping going for the half mile through everything. It was clever of her I suppose, to keep her car where it would not be seen.

She did not know where to turn, so I offered to drive it out of the lane for her. I was bent around the wheel as it was one of those small cars, and my head bounced off the roof. She laughed. I must say it was funny all right, you get in and turn the key and then your head hits the roof as if you were the one started and not the car.

To the Saint John's Road, she said, and pointed me back, saying left and right, the particular way she came, though I knew a shorter way myself. Her map was not local. I estimated by the route she took that she had come twenty miles from Fort Kent, though we were twelve miles as the crow flies from that town. They flew above us black and cawing over the trees.

I switched on the headlights as we approached the edge of the deep woods, stopped and said goodbye and stood in the last sunlight along the wall of green, the brush of the leaves scattering in the high wind like surf.

She said, I can't let you walk those miles. It'll be pitch black.

I've done it many a time, I said, to make her feel at ease. On those nights, with a bottle of something to warm me and a few good cigarettes, I had indeed ventured out in the cool black summer woods.

In any case, I have to drive to the town for some things, I said.

I'll take you.

I hesitated at the offer, going into town with a stranger whose sister said she remembered me. That wasn't a lot to be going with and a long time to be in company.

My name, she said. It's Claire.

The good thing about hearing a name is that it brings the familiar with it, a sound that means someone when you hear it, even if for the first time. And the good thing about wearing a coat for most of the day is that you have what you want in it. We switched places and she covered the gravel road out of the hills, arrived at the crossroads in Saint John, and took a right past the long fields, a few houses and a church.

She said, I knew you lived out here somewhere behind the hills.

So we were coming to it now, why she came, as we sped along the winding road to Fort Kent. Across the river a red tractor in New Brunswick spewed up dust in a potato field. The people of lower New Brunswick were French too, and across the river from Saint Francis was Saint Francois and its own white church spire sticking into the sky. To my right the wide brush of forest led back into the settlements where hunters rented log huts and some families lived. I never met them, but they knew I was where I was and the other way round. That was distance enough for everyone to keep.

Near Fort Kent she slowed past a parked police car and mentioned how isolated we all were up here, even in the town, how important her family was to her and the comfort it brought. I nodded and changed my position on the seat. At the supermarket I was ready to go in when she blurted out that she had been seeing someone recently, but not now, because she needed time to think.

I said nothing as I had not been asked anything, but I should have noted the way she tried to fit a long history into a short trip, how she shared details such as that so easily with a stranger. She brought me back with the groceries as the sun touched the ground and the woods closed in like a zip around us to where the lane narrowed.

You should come again if you'd like, I said, and I glanced a little toward her. It was the way I was then, saying the things a somewhat lonely man will say.

Maybe, she said. Maybe I will.

I walked off into the woods with the brown bag and felt my way by the odd star and a certain amount of memory, stars and memory then, until an hour or so later from the woods I saw the black shape of the barn blot out some of those stars and knew I was home.

I remember thinking as I walked back home that a loss brought her to me, this sudden woman out of the trees, someone she said goodbye to. It made sense, how a lack of something can shake you free of the present and wonder what else there is to be found in life. I admired how she was able to do it, but then the present has the persistence of weeds: it returns every day with the same smell and the same shape and yet you keep expecting something new. Was she expecting that new with me, I wondered.

Now of course I could see the evidence of the seed she had planted: after a brief reference to my school days, she mentioned a man she left behind, knowing that the mind forgets nothing, especially what is left unsaid, and that she could return to the subject of the school later when it would echo against the first reference and seem to make better sense.

I was closing in on her deceit. I placed the rifle inside my coat to keep it warm.

24

ANOTHER TIME SHE SAID THAT SHE KEPT THINKING OF me eating alone, the silence in the house, how the dark nights must affect me. Yes, they did line up in winter, but this was summer and I thought that come the darker months things might be different for me. Then she mentioned I should get myself a dog. I sat in the chair and looked out the window for a minute.

I said, It's been twenty years and probably time for someone else to be living in the house.

You make me laugh when you talk like that, she said.

It was not something I would have done without her: we drove within the hour to the Fort Kent animal shelter in the truck, and I wondered if she minded anyone seeing her with me. She didn't care. The shelter was on the outskirts of town and it was early in the morning. We walked the line of cages. The expressions on the dogs' faces made each one hard to pass. We came to a cage where a small brown terrier was wrapped in sleep but whose eyes flickered open when my shadow crossed them. It straightened up.

That's a dangerous breed, she said.

No, I said, mostly terrier, look at the body. And young.

He had so much spirit and so little time. I agreed to the terms of care and took a leash out of my pocket, from a dog my father once had, I said, and though he cowered at first we walked out with the small fellow pulling me along after I had pulled him, as if to say, I've been waiting, let's go.

I'm sorry I suggested anything, she said. Now when I come I will be facing a pit bull.

We drove back with him between us on the bench seat. Dogs know their fates intimately, and sitting between us in the bench seat of the truck—with me smoking a cigarette out the open window given the occasion—and with the winding roads, this one knew his life had just changed and he was grabbing every moment of it with every glance. When I picked up my mail earlier at the post office I threw it on the seat. Now a bunch of it slid around like so much water and he hopped around the pile between us. I told him I would avoid the letters too. We called him Hobbes.

How quickly successful her plan was.

Dogs have one bond in them, and Hobbes let me know that he had chosen me in ways easily missed: how he came up a few minutes after eating and nuzzled his nose on my leg, as if to say he'd eaten the food. I was of no use to anyone as a father, perhaps that is why I saw the little fellow as the next blessing in line, his need to be cared for, with nothing to give in return but his company.

As for references to my days at school, there was nothing I ever did there apart from turning up and going home, though there was one thing: one day in my final year I did notice a group of boys huddled under a tree during the lunch break. They had a stick and were rattling it in around the leaves. I walked closer and saw a cat trapped on the branch. Now they pelted it with stones: one hit it in the head and drew a line of blood down the ear and mouth. The cat tried to play with the stick in case that would make them like it better, that's what I thought it was trying to do, whatever way the fright was working on its mind. Then it squeezed itself into a ball out of terror and fell, and they were on it, stepping and kicking. I ran the field and then their heads with punches until they spread out. The matter was over as soon as it began, which was just as well as they could have made short work of me had they fought in a unit. One of them had blood on his mouth, another limped holding his knee and saying that I would be sorry, that he had a real father and mother.

The principal was upset that no one noticed anything in a school with so many windows. That is likely what her sister described. Perhaps the local boys turned into men and they were all confederates now so many years after the fact, the settling of an old score in a remote place that manages that kind of thing so well.

I have long believed that the grave is the end of us, and if I did not think so, I might have allowed the killing of Hobbes to pass and allow it some significance in a larger story. But he was a stone, he was stiller than a stone because even a stone moves eventually, kicked by a boot or moved by the weather or a tire, and he was lying packed in clay twenty feet from the cabin, hearing nothing, seeing nothing, tasting nothing, nothing stored in him. That twenty feet might as well have been the universe, it made no difference to him or to me. And he was dead evidently because of some pique, a stored offense over as many years.

I was not going to let that pass.

25

IF CLAIRE HAD A PLAN FOR MY UNDOING, SHE WAS slow and careful in its execution.

Once I was late at the repair shop and when I got home saw the steam and the flicker of candlelight in the bathroom beside the kitchen: she must have poured herself a bath in the antique tub. I had pots in there too with rubber plants and large daisies and beige tile underneath. Within the minute I heard a voice reading poetry and then calling my name, the water may have cooled and I carried some more that had boiled in a large pan on a towel to the door. She was reading a poet from France, I recognized the lines, the rhythms she captured without effort, because the French in her understood the cadences.

I heard her voice: Why don't you pour the hot water into the tub.

It was a voice without a body that drifted through the steam. When I stepped forward, a book emerged from the mist in her hand.

Bring yourself in too, if you want, she said.

I stood inside the door and she asked me to turn the pages for her, an old hardcover, with poems on one side and drawings in thin orange pencil scattered through the pages. I knelt and read in the candles from different poems as she lay in the foam. This poet was killed in the Great War, I said, and there were many in the book who died in that conflict, some known, some not, the words collected from boxes and envelopes, from lonely wives and anguished brothers. She grew still in the hot water surrounded by plants and the perfume of the soap and listened to those voices out of time.

I rested my hand on the edge and wondered if she saw the old English in my face the way I saw the old French in hers, and if such differences mattered. I thought that if she touched me I would disappear too like those vanished men who brought such differences with them into hell.

She said she was tired, asked if she could stay a while.

My bedroom was small and white and the bed-covers were orange and yellow. The mattress leaned over the edge of the wooden frame that lay close to the floor and had a dip in it where I lay every night. She said she could tell I had not had any visitors in a while, and perhaps she wondered if anyone had ever slept in that bed but me. The sheets were clean and whiffed of lavender soap. I had boxes stacked by the walls and a gramophone balanced on three of them over a length of cut carpet, plugged into an outlet shared by the small lamp on another box by the bed. It was my bedroom from the start. My father slept in the room opposite, what was now occupied by shelves and books. We lay together and she slipped the towel off and moved the shirt from my chest.

That night, as in a few other summer nights to come, we warmed each other under the covers, though in the very early hours she rose and went outside to the stove and the chair with the red cushion. I thought I heard her cry, but it may have been the night. I knew what drew her to that chair: you sat in it and wanted to think, you wanted to read something with the whiff of pipe smoke but not from any one thing: even when I held the cushion to my face, the phantom of the pipe produced my father generally about me.

If Claire had a plan for my undoing, she did not stick to it. The following evening she held my hands and placed a small book into them, one I had not seen before, poems by John Donne. On the preface page she had written some lines.

> *All that silence waves across you, Julius, like the long grass.*
> *You make me feel like a poet.*

I was surprised to find myself the subject of such fine words and did not know what to say. She stroked my hands and leaned closer, her whispers soft in the firelight:

You never say how you feel, but I feel affection everywhere in you. Maybe that's what matters, do you think?

If solitude could be measured I suppose it might have been in the way I was happy to see her despite being happy anyway. Now I was more than happy, nothing that I had a word for, to have all this company in my life all of a sudden. She felt to me like those first drops of rain that make you wait in the doorstep with your coat above your head, wondering if this is a small cloud or something longer. In response to her question I simply nodded, because I didn't know what to say. Being given something was new and I hadn't the natural words for the thanks I meant. Her hands slipped away.

With Claire lying beside me that night I heard a fox and plenty of coyotes howling in groups across the fields, and closer to the house the guineas in the trees flapped up into little rows; the roosters babbled in sudden fright at a creature creeping through the undergrowth where they perched, sometimes a scream of pain and fright, something leaped on in the night. The walls sparked and creaked, most of which must have been the wood contracting in the cooler temperatures, but other noises too, things moving, or Hobbes, I wasn't sure.

In the morning I woke with his face in mine: she must have left early for the town.

Love, or words of tenderness and affection, yes, she

had spoken them to me, and I think now that I was meant to respond in kind: yet I was not used to it, how saying a word meant that the feeling was any less or more when it was given a name, but I should have said enough to let her know that I was thankful for her company, that I missed her when she was not about, and if that was love, then we would be fine. Claire never again said something in order to discover what I might say back, or what might be offered in return. I should have known that people can sometimes come close enough to discover that they are strangers.

After that night, she visited less and stayed shorter. The absence of someone comes like a new season, first only in pieces: you see the absence in them long before they leave. In Claire it started with long glances and silence and arrived fully only after she was gone.

26

THAT DAY WE WENT PICKING BLACKBERRIES ALONG
the sloping meadows and wild flowers near Eagle
Lake—we made a trip of it with Hobbes in the truck.
If there is only one field in the world, it must surely be
found in Maine, a hay-green slope to a blue lake that I
knew since a boy: I ran down it and threw a hawthorn
stick from England that my grandfather brought back,
and Hobbes didn't swim after it. We watched it float
away.

Well that's that, I said.

Claire lay on the grass and drew him in pencil and
charcoal. I tipped a bottle of ale sideways for a drink, felt
the sun easy on my face, felt that I was happy. That's it,
she soon said, and handed me the drawing: just one
glance told me the same as a long stare, that she had captured the living dog and his character, matched him to
the whisker. I put the page on the grass without a word,
and afterwards stored it behind the seat for safety.

We drove in the afternoon to the west end of the
valley until the road ran out at the Allagash wilderness.

I parked at the side of a small store by the bridge in front of a large field with fifteen or twenty rusted cars and buses, some from the forties and fifties, clumps of grass showing from the partially open hoods. I left Hobbes in the truck and we walked until I turned and saw that he was a silent waterfall of barking glued to the glass. He noticed what we had not yet seen, what was even now watching us. When we were about to step onto the porch two white wolves jumped down from a bus window and trotted toward us, wolves, the farthest things from men, from any leash that stretches around a property or from a hand.

They moved easily into a run and the crystal blue eyes took up more of their bodies as they covered more ground, a younger one and an older one. I told Claire they were pets, not to worry, though I wasn't sure yet. See, they were slowing down and their tales wagged. When they reached us Claire seemed afraid even though they ignored her and took no actions that indicated they knew she was even there. She shrank back to the truck. One carried a stick in its mouth, a husky and wolf mix, afraid of nothing. They lay on two front seats torn out of a van and placed side by side on the porch facing the road. I rubbed their ears and moved inside: a man came out of a side room on a walking stick wearing a war veteran shirt, and when he heard what I asked for, kindly made me a fresh cup of coffee, and then we talked in the shadows for a while.

Through the door, as I tried the new coffee, I

watched her stare at the sleeping wolves, a stare with absence sown into it, and I decided to keep the card I bought from him, what I had meant to press into her hand to ease the worry I felt in her, a card of a Furbish's Lousewort that grows on both banks of the Saint John River, nowhere else. Above it I had written three letters with the fountain pen:

You.

After that day she did not return.

In the months following I often drove through Fort Kent and saw the smoke winding up from chimneys like ropes attached to the sky, as if the houses hung from them, and I glanced at the windows with their amber lights and imagined what was happening inside, the evening sweaters taken from storage and shaken, the heated wine poured into glasses as the sun grew gold on the trees, the conversation—what it was like, going on late in the year, to be with another person. It took me a long time to understand that she could never have wanted the life I had.

27

THE PRESENTATION OF EVIDENCE WAS OVER, AND THE only one I could find guilty was me: guilty of having brought the accused to it. Now on this first November night of winter I found myself standing inside the circle of trees at such a late hour, holding my midnight court. More geese flew south, long lines in the dark flying low over the trees, scraping them with their peals, scorching the low cloud with their instinct, and still louder as they crossed directly above, fanning the arrow out wide from the tip, streaking through the night sky like broken glass. I should fly with them. This cold.

It was as clear to me as the direction of the geese that Claire could not be the one who did this murder. She may have been careless with men's hearts, but surely she was not cruel. Tonight I should have gone straight back to bed, should have switched off the lamp of memory and remembered nothing. Perhaps I wanted to bring her near to me once more, feel for another hour what I had then.

If the culprit came from that time, there had to be someone else, perhaps the one she left behind, a silent man upset at being abandoned. I searched through the weeks I spent with her, looked for a trace of him, something I may have not noticed.

Somewhere I had not looked.

28

I SAW HIM.

I closed my eyes in the clearing and remembered one evening during the time I was seeing Claire: I was driving home alone when the mist was draped around the church steeple on the other side of the river and was heaviest on the river itself. The lights of a car in New Brunswick driving the other way shone on the silver yarn of the street. The road was sparsely traveled in these conditions. A mile out of town my rear window lit up with the lights of another car. I veered off the road and waited in the shoulder with my engine running and an eye on the mirror trying to see through the mess of the swirling fog on a long road. The car did not pass. Another few miles down the road to the cabin I thought I saw weak headlights again sift in and out of the mist. I drove to the corner and then to the treeline and parked, turned off the lights and waited to see if anyone went by, rolling down the window and looking back in case I missed anything. After thirty seconds a car went by with its lights low, shrouded in fog that peeled off it. I continued up to the cabin until Hobbes bounded down the lane to meet me a hundred yards from the cabin, his eyes shining in the headlights, then the white crest and his tail. He knew the sound of the engine and was the cabin's little alarm clock, had stirred himself into a bark when he heard the truck.

I should have followed that car. I should have overtaken it and slowed it to a stop and walked over to it and tapped on the window. If I had, Hobbes might be alive today. But what did I know then? He was not dead then. It was just a car behind me.

Was that the person who brought a shotgun to these woods a few days ago, the day Hobbes went for his walk? Given what happened as a result, others would be along, no doubt. I opened my eyes and looked into the forest, gripped the rifle and swung at the dark trees.

No men tonight. But they'd be back, yes, those shooters, they would. Some people will not go away, they are too fastened to their habits, they arrive over their own tracks, observe in the same manner, speak the same words, always their undoing. I would meet that driver again. But when I looked down under my feet I did see men: I counted them in the hole with my dog when I looked down to where he was under me, a foot under me as I stood on the slope of absent flowers, I counted as many men packed around him as might have killed him, however many that was or might turn out to be. It was an illusion, a fancy of the brain, since to be accurate those hunters were spread under the forest behind me, but more men were coming out of that forest for me tomorrow, skilled and resourceful men like the ones before, or better this time. The bullet that took his life went through Hobbes and killed a number of them, and there was room in that hole for more. That bullet was not done with its flight yet. Maybe I had not killed them enough.

There was time to fix that. The clearing around me was what the French soldiers called the space between trenches in the Great War: *nomensland*, what the English called *no man's land*, the place you dare not go, because once you cross it you will not come back, not the same man who left.

The night froze me like a stick and shook me at the world, I was that stick being shook at the world. I looked at my hand holding the gun stock. I was the rifle. I was the bullet, the aim, what a word means when it stands on its own. That is what revenge means even if you write it down.

29

THE SNOW WAS THICK AND SAILING ON THE BREEZES. I
went back to the bedroom and pulled the blankets
above me, sank into them and curled up as much as I
could, and the circle made its own heat, enough that
soon I was able to straighten out again. The plastic I had
sealed the panes with still let in enough wind to bend
the candle flame and drive shadows along the wall of
the bedroom, or else the light was shaking itself. But I
felt so numb, as if parts of me had gone away and that
I had shriveled to what could survive, and so I moved
where I remembered my hands were and felt them on
my chest where I had folded them.

Long past midnight, as I lay warm and still,
drifting into the dark, I saw something come for me
out of it.

The wolves who jumped from the bus were running silently at me through the trees, their clear eyes
fixed on the cabin, these two white drops of fur with

blue sights aiming their leaps and strides, how they glided through the stripped rich birch so fast I would only know they passed if my ear were trained to the ground or I saw the snow move at their paws. They flitted through the entire early winter towards me, running in a pair or splitting around trees and fields to gather again into one pace and with one aim. They had covered miles already, loosed from their life in the bus, that last tattered outpost they sojourned in before the wilderness, and as they approached they trained upon me those blue, unwavering eyes.

They knew me now.

PART THREE

November 3rd-5th

30

I WOKE SLOWLY, UNSURE OF THE DAY OR TIME OR WHERE I was until I saw objects I recognized and knew myself to be in the bedroom. The light looked different, the way some days are different right from the start: it must have been the snow reflected into the window from outside, the space around me luminous and hardly made of objects at all.

I heard a voice beside me, a human voice formed around words other than my own thoughts, and I turned my head to the shortwave radio, still warmed up to a Canada station from the night before. I lay under the blankets and listened. True enough, snow showers for today, but later something ominous, a story told in numbers from Quebec and north of there, the temperatures ahead of and behind a much colder front, a hard line drifting south with wind and steadier snow and then a numbing cold.

The announcer stated that it was Friday, the morning of the third, the first weekend then of what was to be the real winter—a day, two at most until the weather came upon these woods with its wide brush of paint, in a single pass the season of coats.

I rose and made for the cold shirt hanging on the doorknob, pulled the pants up my legs and wended my way to the fire, shoving logs together over paper and setting a shaking match to it. The icy fog of breath rose also, wrung out of me like a spirit. As a child I'd often wondered if I was losing myself into the air on such mornings as these. I was slow today, as if catching up with myself or waiting for my senses to come along, and I felt pain where I went to sleep with none.

I pierced a slice of bread with the long fork and held it against the flames, and afterwards wandered around the house sipping mouthfuls of hot tea around the toast. My mind was as blank as the land outside, though I had thoughts of the writing on the poster and of how far things had come in a few days after a life-time of relatively nothing. I thought of Hobbes, my first weekend without him.

With little to place my eyes on while I drank, I picked out the Shakespeare list from between the books and went down to D. Strange, I could remember writ-ing these particular words, the smell in the room when I wrote them, what I saw when I wrote them, the feel-ing in my hand as I scratched out the letters, what I was wearing and how small and safe the world was, the warm fire, my father's gentle assurance that books mat-tered, that reading them mattered more. Now that the world had gone to hell and was never coming back, that memory seemed all the more important. Everything was in the books, look at all the books, a life's worth, those living walls around me.

There were four words, though the list might have been compiled over two days and not one because of the different inks, blue and black, for the first one and last three: *Disponge*, to squeeze out, and after a space, the next three in black: *distraction*, a troop of isolated soldiers; *discase*, to undress; *declined*, meaning fallen. It was nothing but a coincidence that the words from that section seemed to fall happily on the subject of the day, that the morning seemed intent on disponging all the available snow from the sky and sprinkling it upon the yard, the barn, the flowerbeds, the woodpile, and the porch around the door of the cabin, as if I had been writing for times ahead and not practicing a language long dead.

Claire was still on my mind, lay there freshly upon my other thoughts now that I had seen her yesterday, and twice for that matter, or three times if my thoughts counted, and I wondered if she lived in Fort Kent now. Strange that you can sleep with someone and a few months later not know the first thing about them, never mind years.

Whatever my intention, it was as yet a haze, but I warmed up the truck, poured hot tea into a thermos, and with a book of verse, a list slipped inside it, along with the rifle and the telescopic sight, I headed along a set of tracks on the road east that would eventually bring me to her town if I kept driving, and soon was, churning my way easily through the thin white linen of a countryside featureless except where birds poked out pools of water. I was unsure of my plans for the day, why I was driving with a rifle and to what end, and felt much less sure when I saw a man standing solitary in the middle of nowhere, a man who appeared to raise his arm is if ordering back a tide.

31

HE STOOD ON THE ROAD ABOUT A MILE AHEAD, A DOT in the glazed powder. I watched him through the glass and slowed, but it was still only a matter of seconds before I reached him and whatever he had to say to me.

This is no flat country, except in one place where the paved road to Fort Kent evens out over a couple of miles, and in the normal course of events if you are out on a journey and happen to see someone walking you have time to prepare a conversation if you have a mind for one, or a salute if it is to be a passing without words. Any questions are proper and thoughtful and answered in kind.

Yes, closer now, and there he was for definite. He appeared to face in my direction as he saw my truck approach. I lowered the window with my left hand as I slowed, wondering what sort of conversation was to be had today, but I did not really have time to come to terms with what he might be doing out here in the middle of nowhere. My decision to take a drive was sudden, and even a random talk might demonstrate that, why I was driving, where I was going. Now in the last fifty yards the windshield wipers pushed aside the spray of washer fluid and he stood clearer, a man in a police jacket, his free hand on a waist holster, a revolver. I saw the other hand rise again and unfurl to an arm: this fellow wanted me to stop.

32

HE STEPPED ASIDE AFTER I PULLED UP AND THE BRAKES squealed in the thin air, appeared to be someone ill at ease in himself or annoyed in general: even his skin looked like a large raincoat thrown hastily across him. The evidence suggested he did not like doing this, being here, and his voice rang on the sharp side of friendly:

You haven't seen anything up there, have you?

I fingered the key, and as the engine died the silence crowded around my first words to him:

Seen what then?

I wrapped my forearms around the steering wheel and leaned down to the window at the same time as he leaned in. His face was a cloud of breath.

Shots, suspicious activity, he said. A few miles around you up there. Anything?

I said, Plenty of hunters wandering about, so you get the shots coming across the woods.

He nodded when I said that, as if he had expected an answer such as I gave.

But nothing else, I said, apart from the winter coming in general. It's mostly quiet.

His hand still rested on the holster, though he made a show of draping the fingers over his belt in a relaxed manner. I did not know specifically what he was looking for because I had no television and no way of knowing what they knew and if any of what they knew had pointed them here.

Is that right, he said. He was chewing something, gum most likely, and his eyes covered the truck cabin like a sheet blowing this way and that on a line. I waited for him to finish. He had probably spent twenty minutes and more standing before I appeared on the horizon and he wanted to make some conversation out of it, seeing as the next driver might still be a town away. Nevertheless I decided that my best words at this point should be stuffed with plenty of nothing else to say between them.

Can you contact us if you hear anything out of the ordinary? We've had reports.

I will.

He looked up and saw me watching him.

And you have a book, he said.

I looked down to the sonnets on my lap, the list of Shakespeare words folded inside.

In case I have a few minutes in the café between errands, I said.

What's it about, he said.

It's a book of sonnets. Poetry that is.

He pursed his mouth. What's your favorite poem then?

At that second the wind blew in a burst of snow, a few flakes, and dusted the seat with them. His question was thoughtful and not one that could be answered lightly, even if the circumstances, as they did now, required it, since people who ask questions for a living or out of habit take offense when those questions are left unanswered.

I like them all, it depends.

On what?

On what the day brings.

I decided it was time to go or for him to ask me to get out of the truck. I turned the key and the engine ran. He glanced at the seat again and coughed.

It occurred to me that he might ask to search the car and would find the Enfield and sight I'd hidden behind the seat. An impulse had me place them there instead of on the seat as usual, lucky for me.

He stepped back and put both hands on his gun belt.

So if I asked you to get out of the vehicle and stand there, he pointed down beside his boots, you wouldn't be able to recite me a couple of lines and call it your favorite poem.

I did not like his sudden tone with me.

I said, For most days I would be able, but not as a rule for all days, speaking louder above the engine hum. In any case I was not good at quoting anything beyond a few short words, not having the capacity for such feats of mind.

He separated his feet to shoulder width and shrugged. If this were a planned stop and they'd been waiting for me I was a sitting duck and would not survive a gun draw. He'd fire on me at close range as I was grappling for the rifle behind me, an awkward death. I placed my foot on the pedal and handled the gear stick into first.

We have ourselves a man of letters, he said and smiled, looked to his side, the direction I was going in.

Thank you for your cooperation.

I was being sent away. That was fortunate for me. I drove off with a wave and watched him all the way along the straight past of the road till he was a man shrunk once more to a small mark shrouded in engine smoke on the side mirror. Then I wondered why I hadn't seen a police car, not even parked off the road where there wouldn't even be space for one, and since under no circumstances had he walked out here, they must have dropped him off. But that made no sense either.

After the first bend I pulled over and took the rifle from the back and laid it out on the seat. I considered the situation as the truck chugged and flakes blew across the hood. If they were closing in then I must act. I could turn around and shoot him from almost anywhere, but if he had been dropped off there to do a checkpoint such a shooting would invite that much more attention as the search for him began. In any case he had certainly not killed my dog of late and so I had no quarrel with him. Still I decided to think about it some more seeing as he had moved into this part of the world: I took the rife out of the cloth and walked to the side of the truck out of sight of a passing car and farther to the bend. But now the man was not standing where I left him. That was fairly quick of him. I waited a few minutes just in case he was relieving himself, went for the book and opened it where I had a leaf inserted, a poem about love and such matters, and sat by the wheel with the rifle perched.

The wind swept up the snow a field away and rolled past a moose standing still. A large high bird curved and straightened out in the bluster, eyes steady on some creature no doubt: their eyesight burned the impurities from ordinary vision and presented them with the smallest movement, the tiniest flicker, even the intent of a snow rabbit or small owl to cover an open stretch across the white, its last run.

When I got back to the bend with the rifle inside my coat I saw two red dots pulling up over the hill a good mile off, the tail lights of a car. He had been picked up, but going in a different direction, the back roads. Then it was clear, they were setting up check-points at unusual places to pare down to a final point, closing in on the whereabouts of the killer. Or the point was them sticking a pin on the map of the county and hoping. I toyed with idea of a fast shot, a mile about, not out of the question, but hardly time for two shots. And there'd be no hiding two men anyway, never mind a car off a narrow road.

I left the rifle back in its cloth on the seat and set off again. In addition to the book and the weapon I had brought an index card and pencil, a kind of bait, for I had not forgotten that there was a writer in Fort Kent who had plenty to say to me evidently.

33

I DROVE THE LONG WAY AND THE ONLY WAY IN WINTER,
through the towns of Fort Kent and Frenchville, then
south to St. Agatha, passing the slow trucks that spread
salt and ploughed the snow aside, their wipers and
headlights on. The entire sky had fallen and collapsed
into sludge. You could lose the place where the sun
hung on a day like this except for the wind that herd-
ed the clouds from occasional patches

The weather forecasters down in Bangor always
point to Caribou on the map and refer to it as "up
there," but that town is forty miles south of us, and we
are also a good four hours north of Montreal. Fort Kent
is the most north you can live in the continental United
States and be in any town: people hanging their wash-
ing in long back yards can see the televisions flickering
in the living rooms of people in Saint Clair, New
Brunswick. If that isn't enough you can also speak
French all day long if you want, even the English in you
has run out by the time you make it this far. A small few
thousand year-rounders live here, and the main street

twists along a few restaurants, banks, a supermarket, building supply store, auto shop, pharmacy, a motel, and then opens out on both sides west into the wider Saint John Valley, the fields and the forest, the road following the river turn for turn, like dancers. I stopped at a station off the highway. A logging truck maneuvered in the parking area, and two men in red gear and flannel shirts held steaming coffee by the wall outside the restaurant where it was warmer, especially now that some blue had broken out briefly in the sky.

I passed them with a nod.

It'll melt now, one of them said to me, for the day and some of tomorrow.

Expect so, I said, and entered, felt the blast of hot air and the smell of more hot coffee and fried bacon. I did not want much, some tea and a cheese sandwich. The restaurant was busy, and this morning, hours after the first snowfall, the snowboarders no doubt soon arriving, though not as many as in parts south and west, and the place would fill with noisy families, not the hard men and women who sat here today, the ones with long journeys fixed permanently in their eyes, the long-distance men.

A very light snow from the cloudy part of the sky brushed the air and swept the parking area as a truck drove in with antlers attached. Two men got out and walked in, thick arms, caps down to cigarettes without smoke. They eased into their table and made their orders with a nod. Snatches of their talk drifted

through the clang of cutlery and the orders, the
coughing and sneezing, the drone of the television up
on the wall unit:

I bagged a big buck and had him strapped to the
back in under fifteen minutes.

Yeah? I took this one black bear that came at me
and moved off again like it knew. I opened up with the
Winchester, dropped it like a sack.

Some of the locals, they're harvesting a lot of bears
up there on the border.

Then their voices dropped and they leaned
together. I had to turn my head to hear the whispering
above the clank of dishes:

No, don't know what's happened either. No sign
of him these past three days. And then the other two. I
tell you this, something's wrong. Men don't go off missing in groups without sight nor sound.

One of them lit his cigarette and saw me staring
at him and I looked up to the television where on the
screen a rifle was superimposed over a red question
mark.

And now, reporting from Fort Kent: three missing
hunters and two families in a desperate limbo. What has
happened in the North Woods? Where have these men
disappeared to?

Three photographs popped up on the screen. Yes,
there they were, and up last the bow hunter, the skinny
one. The reporter said that two of them were family
men from Frenchville, whom I knew to be the two

recent friends now lying in the truck in the woods, and the first in the shooting order lived in Fort Kent. Two had children but not the skinny, who was not married. I felt my heart drop at the children item. The little fellows, no father now; there was no need for that, and why in heaven's name would a man need to go hunting when he had a child at home? And why go hunting and near my cabin? Why shoot a dog or associate with a dog shooter? That's what happens when you do that kind of thing, isn't it just. Harvest, that hunting term, it sounded more like what you do with crops and didn't seem all that bad a thing to do, which is what I was doing anyway. Get them where they don't expect, isn't that what hunting is all about, the art of the hunt? You hide and let them have it if they have it coming.

You should all have been more careful. I said to the crossbow man, You came to shoot in the woods, but the woods shot back.

I wanted to feel sympathy, but sympathy was driving ahead of me and I'd be behind it in a few minutes, as soon as I finished the sandwich cradled in my hands, which were shaking. My hands never shook, even when I was nervous. A state trooper car pulled up outside as I munched.

Two troopers got out and came in and went up to the counter, their revolvers shooting a stripe down the side of the trousers, and they opened not a newspaper but a map, the county it looked like, with some circles drawn. They didn't have to ask, the waitress put coffee in front of them, and they looked up as the television news item on the missing hunters continued.

I went to the bathroom and saw as I passed them a circle on the map around McLean Mountain and the Back Settlement south of St. Francis, on the river, a few hundred yards from the border. A fifty-square mile circle at first glance, and three arrows coming at it from different directions. They were triangulating.

Fair enough, that was to be expected. But as I washed my hands in the soap and cold water I realized I would have to be more careful if there were ever any confrontation again, mighty careful, otherwise those arrows might take a better aim and finally point to the cabin and in the window from every direction. But then my present journey might help aim them the wrong way. I paid my check and said good morning to the officers, who smiled a greeting back.

I got in the truck and drove away with a fresh cup of coffee to go. Hot tea was good for a gentle, steady, reliable life, the broad arc of the afternoon, that sort of thing, and I brought some for later, but for ten minutes that followed, I needed the coffee to surge my blood awake and keep me alert for locations. A car with skis on the roof rack passed me, going in the opposite direction. People dressed in yellow coats and hats, even in the car. They were that eager to hit the slopes, and it was cold, getting colder. I wondered why I chose St. Agatha instead of the woods around my house, where Hobbes was shot and my reasons for taking action were more defensible: I knew it had nothing to do with Claire being from there, and anyway, she lived in Fort Kent now it seemed. I was not driving into St. Agatha with a rifle looking for Claire.

34

I ARRIVED IN ST. AGATHA AT ONE-THIRTY IN THE afternoon and made a left for the east side of the lake south of town, the wilder part, and parked off the road, and with the rifle slung and the book under my coat and the thermos in my right pocket I walked to the nearest tree with a tree stand on it, one that bordered a field and offered an excellent field of fire. The woods were sparse here, more potato fields than trees, but bird and deer hunters would no doubt be active here, and possibly that fellow who was commentating on the poster.

Wouldn't be long now, not on a day like this, with the blue breaking out all over the sky and deer tracks peppering the woods. I leaned the rifle on the railing and opened the book of sonnets and poured a mouthful of Earl Grey onto my tongue—nothing like that first bite of sun on your face in the cold weather. But I had other matters on my mind, drawings and lines of statistics, ordinance and such.

A book I once read said that war snipers in northern climates wore white for camouflage. This was a detail I remembered before leaving the cabin this morning, when I wrapped the barrel of the Lee Enfield in a white blanket to keep it warm and the gun invisible against the snowy bark of the tree. That's why when I was up in the tree I also covered myself partly with the same blanket, the eyes cut out so I could see. From a distance the stand would appear unoccupied.

I took the Aldis telescopic sight from the leather carrying case and attached it to the mount. The curious thing about many of the telescopic sights used with the Enflields in World War One was that they were attached left of the bore, forcing the shooter to aim with his left eye or move his cheek off the stock to sight with the right, losing the tight wedge against the rifle necessary for a steady aim.

I swept the field, moving the range drum on the sight, and saw how the sight seemed to gather the available light and create a luminous halo around objects. Now to make a range card, the way my father taught me, to help me judge distance before a shot and allow for elevation and bullet drop. I set an index card against my knee and drew expanding circles radiating from my position, four circles, each representing a distance of one hundred yards. Then I marked a tree that stood approximately half way between the first and second circle and added a simple drawing of the electricity pole that stood twenty yards on my side of the third circle.

With that done, I threw a piece of the card in the air and watched it fall to get a sense for wind speed, the windage, though you can never tell with gusts, and today was a day for sudden blows, but on this day they would all blow from left to right.

Some live their lives in preparation. A time comes when what's left to do is wait.

I sat still and rested my eyes as much as I could. If a time came when I had to aim, the eyes can quickly tire and must be rested. After a short while, an hour at most, I observed a shape walk with a rifle slung over the shoulder, skirting the line of the woods across the field, a distance of four hundred and fifty yards. I brought the rifle up and sighted him.

In 1914 the Germans discovered that the best place to aim at a human body was the teeth, a miss six inches up or down still gives you a mortal shot; and if aiming for the area between the head and waist, you have two feet down by one foot across to hit and should try for the middle.

The man moved out of the tree line and into the field. I took my gloves off and bunched them against the stock and leaned my cheek against them to wedge the gun into my shoulder. I closed my left eye and opened my right in the sight, found him, zeroed up half an inch for distance and made a best guess for wind, aiming off a bit to the left, and took a deep breath, letting it out and pulling the trigger, and the man in the sights stopped and spun half way around and fell on his back.

I kept an eye on the shape that was now lying in the field.

The biggest mistake a sniper makes, and unusually the last, is to check on his shot, to get up and stare, to come to the window, the ledge. The novice can't resist looking out the window or peeking above the wall to confirm a kill. Which is what the other side wants, because they have a number of rifles pointed at that window or that wall and will wait for two or three hours for the split second when the face appears up for a view, and that half second is all they need to shoot a bullet into that face. So after the report died away into the white wasteland I froze and kept the rifle parallel for a full five minutes, using my knee as support and opening my right eye occasionally to check on the shape in the snow. Most of those five minutes I sat with my eyes closed, bunched up on the stand.

The shape did not pick itself up and walk away, and from every side came nothing but silence and wind brushing snow along the tops of the trees. The least I could do was approach and ask about Hobbes, so I packed up and walked across the field, past the tree and the pole. It was a long way to the man declined in the snow. After a hundred yards I noted that he was lying by a pool, after two hundred a red pool, and after three hundred a red pool from his head. At four hundred yards from the tree where I sat and aimed the shot, I stood beside him, the drawing of Hobbes in my hand, but there would be no questions today. If this were the shooter of a dog, he brought that to his grave. He had spun out of his left boot when shot, but how I could not figure, unless he had not laced it up properly.

I pulled his license out of his wallet: he was local, one of them alright, the Fort Kent crowd spreading out after me. That was good then, to bring them farther out here, the wrong way. And everywhere now I sensed them closing in. I dragged him inside the treeline and flopped him down scooped some dead leaves and branches over him. At the edge of the woods was best, with all the brush and tangled brush. He would be okay here. I noticed a car drive by, then another, and thought it best not to stay in the area. I could depend on most people not noticing what was immediately in front of them, but you never know. There's always one.

At the last moment I said anyway: Did you shoot my dog? Do you know I shot you? The shot caught you unawares, you declined like the others, and that's your blood disponging.

Then I said, Did you write on that poster? Was that your hand?

He said nothing, at least the bits of him I could see through the dressing of undergrowth I put across his body, so I wasn't entirely addressing him then. If he were the writer, he was not going to write anything again: if I put up a new poster and it wasn't written on, I might have got my man. If he were in Fort Kent to write on a poster, then he might as easily have gone anywhere hunting, including around the cabin. It was advisable for that reason to have spread the net like this to catch him. And he came with a fancy rifle, a Browning Gold model, very expensive, very clean, polished like a boudoir mirror, one of those guns from the magazine. He must have read the advertisements too.

Possibly it was the caliber that knocked his boot off, or him out of it.

My father once sat me in front of him, a .303 cartridge held in his hand to the light, long as a finger it was, and it looked as if he had six fingers, I said.

This is not a finger, Julius, he said. It spins through the rifle bore and travels at over 2500 feet a second. It penetrates the bones and veins and muscle like wet cucumber. Some Germans we shot in Holland at a hundred yards, we found them later cracked and broken, as a good part of the body sometimes won't stay intact against one of these.

You mean this bullet blows people up, I said.

That is essentially what it does, he said.

On the drive back from St. Agatha I saw more police cars at one end of Fort Kent's main street stopping drivers, asking questions, searching trunks, but only those leaving town. I parked behind the supermarket, close to three o'clock, put the weapon and other items behind the seat, and tacked the new poster on the wall in the usual place using a blue nail someone left sticking in the noticeboard, this time a 4x5 inch index card, the same size as my range card: DOG SHOT, Information to J. Winsome, P.O. Box 271, Fort Kent.

I walked to the diner, where the waitress touched my shoulder with her voice and then her smile:

And what can I get you today?

Coffee, I said as I went to the small table by the window behind the large floor plant, a palm, like the one I had in the cabin by the bookshelves, the warm books in the window sunlight.

I must discase myself, I said to her as I took my coat off. She nodded and said,

Yep, that's the coffee right there.

When she left me, and I was sure I wasn't being observed, I opened the carrying case and lifted the telescopic sight to my right eye and brought it to the noticeboard two blocks down, ranged the focus, and put the sight on my lap. Every couple of minutes I trained it through the café window to catch any anonymous writers. The waitress saw me and wandered over with her coffee pot and asked me who I was spying on, then laughed.

I nodded. I am testing a very old sight. The optics.

Well as long as there's no gun under it in here, I'm fine with that.

I smiled. Always having to have their word in, some people, and I kept my smile until she went away, and then I brought the sight again to my face.

There, a man with a scarf around his head leaning

to the wall with a pen or some instrument. I tried for more detail with my finger, turning the dial. There had been shots with Enflields up to a thousand yards. It was not an impossible shot at all, especially if along a street, walls on each side, a corridor to help shepard the bullet.

Suddenly the sight went out of focus, a black cloud crossed it, pale on top, and then a tap sounded on the window, another when I pretended not to hear and didn't move. After a few seconds I realized that freezing did not bring safety or invisibility, as the person evidently knew I was sitting at the window and was probably in fact on the other side of it. I removed the sight and blinked: Claire stood on the pavement outside, wrapped in gloves and a scarf except for her bare left hand touching the glass, the glove held in her right, as if she were leaning on the window with her fingertip. If she were an adversary and we in the open I might not have survived the next few seconds. She had stood so close I did not see her, and I determined not to forget that lesson.

Her face was shaped a pear in the scarf but enough to recognize. I saw her say my name, heard the last syllable of it, us, the sound muffled as though she stood at some distance, like a shout across a wide stretch of woodland. I sat holding the sight and made no movement. She had spied me in the act, and now she passed along the window and walked into the diner, across the floor and into the reflection of the same window up to my table, ignoring the waitress who followed her with a coffee pot.

Julius, she said.

I turned until she was real in front of me. Yes?

What's that? She pointed to my lap.

Optics, I'm having them looked at today. Down at the gun shop.

Troy, she said, you know Troy?

I saw him with you, I said. I was there, if you remember.

She sat opposite me, unfurled the scarf off her head, and I saw the full face that lay beside me on many mornings when I woke, a very happy season.

What are you doing, Julius? It's just that Troy says, I mean he's talking about where they think the killer is operating, or where they think he lives.

Killer, I said.

They found a body, she said.

35

It was my father who taught me basic rifle skills. The war stories came mostly from my grandfather and contained other rifle skills buried in their telling, lessons he learned about shooting under pressure and being shot at. As my father relates it, my grandfather came home from World War One and was fine for twenty years; then one afternoon, for no evident reason, he broke down and said he had seen the faces of his victims in his dreams for some weeks past, and not only their faces but also the children they never had, crowding the edge of the dreams, legs and arms sneaking into the picture. After some time, when the trouble did not disperse in him, a doctor was mentioned. Perhaps, it was suggested to my grandfather, he was suffering from shell shock.

No, my grandfather said. This is no shell shock. I was not generally under artillery fire.

My father explained to him that he might not have seen the faces of many people he shot as a sharpshooter since they were often a hundred yards and more away, and at that distance the faces were a plate, no eyes or expression a human would have. But there was no reassuring him, my father said to me, and my grandfather grew quiet after that, grew haunted, hollow, his eyes blacker, as if looking through sights at things a long way off.

I cannot believe how unlucky your grandfather was to have been caught up with like that, he said to me.

Caught up with? I said.

Yes, they caught up with him. You see it from battle.

My father was so sparing in his words you had to add water to them before they swelled into a sentence you could understand.

I said, From battle?

He thought some more and put down his book to say what he had to say.

That's it, a gun leaves a battle loaded with dead men. Your grandfather must have seen so many times their faces through the telescopic sights, the surprise on the face of the man he shot that *he* was shot, that he was shot and not the man next to him or someone way down the line or on another battlefield altogether, so much surprise that those men crawled twenty years toward him with their fingertips, and when they got to him he was lying asleep in his bed, so they pressed those fingers into his dreams and punctured them like wet jelly, entered into those dreams and stood up and he saw them, all of them, in that jelly, in their uniforms, sick to their boots of the long journey into his dreams. And then they pointed those fingers at him and said, Remember me? You killed me.

Hearing that, I realized that the medals and the rifle were not the only things my grandfather brought back from the war. The men he killed dragged themselves across seas and rivers, roads and hills, an inch a day, unerring as to the compass that pointed to my grandfather, and when they found him, they must have smelled his dreams, tasted them too, ate them until they were the only dream that was left in his head, the only one his sleep could produce, and so he soon stopped sleeping and spent the nights with his eyes open in the dark.

To my knowledge my father never fired a single killing shot out of that gun. Perhaps he did not want to have any ghosts come after him if they heard a familiar sound, the last sound they may have heard in their lives, even if it wasn't a gun he fired at them, or his father fired at them for that matter. The English sniper's gun came with spirits attached, following it like a wake behind a ship, the water coiling in white streamers. My father had been a regular paratrooper in the last year of the second great war and did little that could be called sniping, mostly running and firing, more running and firing, a lot of ducking, more running and firing. Of the war he said little other than that the destruction was complete in most villages along the way to the Rhine, rubble where there used to be windows, rubble where there used to be people. And that destruction cured him of triggers completely.

For my part, I had discharged the Enfield twice before the recent events. Once I shot a wounded fowl at my father's direction, and later, the following winter, a fox that limped into the clearing, bleeding from what I believed was a bear wound. The fox did not run when I approached, and when I saw his condition, he still did not move, and when I brought out the gun, he looked at it and me. The shot filled the forest and drove the fox to the ground. There is little honor in pain or in enduring it, and less honor in ending it. In truth I thought of that fox for many a night after and hoped the best for him, if beyond the body there really is a place you can survive.

What I mean by all of this is that shooting did not come easy to me. I dreaded the kick and smell, the dead thing at the other end, torn.

36

STANDING UNDER THE STRONG BULBS OF THE
diner, Claire stared at me as if delivering that word,
Body—what they found—with her eyes as well as
mouth.

Sometimes your eyes get full quickly like a pint of
water poured into a thimble and you can't see everything at once, you have to choose what to look at. A
patrol car drew up outside as she mentioned the body,
but I kept my eyes focused on Claire, which was hard
to do, as I kept seeing the months I spent with her,
thinking what her eyes must have seen in me, wondering how whatever she saw was ever enough at all, even
for that amount of time, how her lips felt on mine, the
touch of her hands on my shoulders.

The door of the patrol car opened. I thought of
Hobbes, that it had been worth it if the person who
took his life was gone himself, worth it even if now my
wrists were chained and I was led away while Claire
watched, and if she had given me away. Only someone
close can betray you in the end.

She sighed and shook her head, looked down and away from me, to my relief.

They've drawn a box from Fort Kent to Allagash, and inside it another box up around McLean Mountain. That's where you live, Julius.

I said, Indeed it is.

I watched a pair of police boots walk up to the window and stop even at the glass, angled the way men stand who are authorities.

She said, Please be careful, Julius. Are you sure that everything is okay up there?

Why wouldn't it be okay? I am not a hunter.

I divided my sight between her and the boots.

Troy says they're looking up your way, I heard him mention it today. I haven't said anything, I never would, not to him or anyone.

I took my eyes off the boots. What would you say, Claire?

Nothing. I mean, nothing.

The police boots stood there in the bottom of my eyesight, tips pointed toward the diner in a gathering light afternoon fog. Claire looked up and nodded at the window, stood and put her hand on my shoulder: Take care, Julius.

I did not look up when Claire left the table, and the boots shifted and went back to the police car. A very intense man, this Troy. I hoped his intensity would keep him looking too hard for me and miss what was in front of him, as had just happened to me not five minutes ago.

Then I wondered if it was all over; with the body found, they must have discovered more than just the one, surely, in the woods and close to the cabin, and now Troy was waiting outside to make the arrest of Julius Winsome, late companion to a dog. No more looking, looking is done for today—we found you. I wondered if I shouldn't go out and make conversation with him, close the distance to him, he wouldn't expect that, and be cheerful on top of it, catch him doubly unawares with something like, How now, Troy, and what cheer?

Someone in the diner said for everyone to be quiet as the waitress leaned up on her toes to turn the knob on the television, and out poured a reporter's voice, a microphone and some woods, a moving camera at a treeline, some yellow tape and flashing lights. You can't go anywhere without the televisions. The café filled with the loud wind in the reporter's microphone, the volume way up, and no one said a word or made a sound among the tables, everyone froze. I saw snow on the ground, so it was today, it was live. I thought I remembered the run of the same trees across the skyline when I took the long shot, so that would have to mean this morning.

Friends, the reporter said, had found the body, the long-distance body, the new one, but those last ones were my words, and thankfully I said them low and no one heard me. They had gone out hunting with him late this morning, the reporter said, and heard a shot and thought it his, but when they had not seen him for a while they back-tracked and eventually found him in the brush.

That detail told me the news item must be dealing with this morning's event, if only they would pull back on the camera shot so I could see the bigger picture, recognize the woods. That was a relief, my cabin was still safe at least.

The mouth on the microphone continued, The friends stumbled on to a terrible sight, the body of their friend buried under leaves and branches, as if stored, shot only minutes before, according to police sources at the scene.

Yes, but did they see anything, a person walking away with a rifle? And where was Troy now? I had to keep an eye everywhere it seemed to me.

The camera pulled back. Then a banner appeared at the bottom of the screen, Long Lake, St. Agatha. The relief in me when I saw that it was this day's man and not the previous men who were lying not one mile from where I lived and who would have pointed the way to my cabin even in death. The television showed my footprints in the snow but blurred from the wind and too deep for detail, and the reporter said that the victim, whom police described as a local hunter, was shot from a half mile away, shot through the teeth, killed instantly, an expert shot. That seemed insensitive, I thought, that kind of detail. What if the family were watching? What was she thinking? Then the reporter held her hand to her ear as if listening and went pale and flustered, and the camera moved to an officer of the law standing beside her.

Particularly savage, said a police captain to the camera. Appalling, he said.

A fast world I lived in. An hour at most, and the reports already widespread.

Then more news flashed across the screen, breaking news, a gravelly voice, police now saying that a serial killer, a sniper, could be loose in and around Fort Kent and the western St. John Valley.

I checked outside: that swirling vague fog, but no Troy, no police. They were waiting out of sight or they weren't waiting at all. No point in thinking like a victim, and if they were there, fine. Time to go home.

I slipped the sight into its case and went outside, went right for the supermarket and my truck; along the way I passed a boy and his mother, tipped my hat and smiled at the young fellow, and he smiled back. I sensed they were without, and if I had some money I would have bought the child a toy, or something at least. The festival tree grew brighter as I approached, lit the pavement and my boots, but I sensed no heat in the light, they were just the decorations.

Already the locals had gathered outside the supermarket, a constable there too in the middle, nodding and holding up his arms and then shaking his head and criss-crossing his arms in a big no.

What about the law, why can't you catch him, one

man said. Two men walked out of a side street, large men, heavy with big coats and guns. One waved his in the air and said, We're being shot at and no one is doing anything.

The policeman said, We're trying, it's all woods up here and you know that very well, Pascal, and we don't know for sure that anyone else has even been shot. This is early on.

What do you think, the gun waver shouted back at the policeman.

I think you need to calm down, the policeman said. I think you all need to move on and stop blocking the thoroughfare.

I stood beside the crowd and tried to read the poster through all the shoving and the consternation in the cold mist. People get upset very quickly, the citizenry teems along, never more than an inch from their passions. One dead body half an hour away and everyone is up in arms.

There you have it, I could not read the poster, but I could see some new writing on it, that man had penned something for sure: a black spider of words. Just too many bodies in the way. Didn't want to be obvious, peering at it up close. I decided to go back to the diner and wait, let them disperse like snow in a bluster. First I put the sight back in the truck, no point in carrying that around and asking for trouble.

Since I left, the diner had filled with pedestrians come in for the reports, two extra televisions had sprouted, one on a table they cleared for it, so different people stared at different televisions. I stood between the two television tables, looking for my waitress. She was standing with her tray extended in front of her, mouth open. The entire place was silent, and I could have been standing in the silent forest with all those straight, standing bodies and the sitting ones like trees around me.

Can I have a cup of coffee, I said to no one in particular.

Someone looked me up and down as if I had done something terrible. All I had done was ask for coffee. I looked for a table, but the only one available was the table with the television on it, so I sat behind it on a chair I dragged up. Now everyone was looking at me but not at me. That was strange, that I was in the best hiding place, the best camouflage in the countryside, better than any hole in the deep forest. I was sitting behind a television with everyone staring.

I passed the next hour listening to words like news, fast and anxious, the mounting evidence, the fading light in St. Agatha, a high-caliber bullet, battle-munitions variety, victim killed instantly, and then, police have a lead, some footprints. I could not see the images that went with the reporter's voice, but I had seen those footprints before anyway. I leaned with my chin in my hand, with an ear to the details. Police have a lead indeed. She was not telling the truth, I could tell because the tone of her voice changed, the timbre.

They were telling her to say that, to rouse the prey.

When I felt it was time, I rose and walked away, and to everyone in the café it must have seemed that I rose out of the television itself and walked toward them saying, I am the killer of all these men. Can't you see me? Outside, I noted how empty the streets were all of a sudden. Maybe because it was dark and there was a shooter of men abroad. The supermarket had closed early and the lights were out around it, so I had to lean close to the noticeboard, and the writing was tiny: *Guess who shot your dog.*

Of the writer I saw no sign, but the writing was his, the geography of the D was the same as the other notes on the posters. So I had the bastard. Shooting the other man today was not justified in that case. But he was ruled out now, as well as any others not directly in the woods around the cabin. So from now on, if there were any more incidents, they would only happen there, even if it invited attention in the long run. And I committed to memory the scarf's appearance. I would know him again.

Beside my index card hung a sheet on which someone had written in black marker: "Wanted, the shooter of Henri Dupre on Long Lake. Information to Fort Kent or St. Agatha Sheriff's Office." Not an official poster, that one. An angry citizen. I thought of drawing a bullseye around the word SHOOTER with an X through it, but there was no reason for doing it, no point in that kind of cruelty.

I took my card off the board. The snow had come on again, blowing hard and thick. Soon it would be time for chains on the tires, a shovel in the back to dig my way out of embankments and when I skidded off the road, especially up in the woods. That time of year now, and so suddenly. Five, six months of it coming, lined up.

That morning before taking the road to St. Agatha I had put Hobbes' things away. I could not place my eyes anywhere in the cabin and not see him, and what was there and what was gone kept colliding in me so much that I sat for a while and determined to move them, his nest and brush and everything, away into another room, the one opposite my bedroom, where my father used to sleep. What to do with them besides, the rope he pulled on, the knot I tied to hold it the better with. A small broad-chested terrier is not at his happiest until tugging at the other end of a rope, a growl clamped around his teeth with tail wagging that says, I'm playing. If I had the presence of mind I would have buried the rope with him, though I felt now there would be no waking for him in another life, no toy to pick up again, it was this world or none for him. What he loved in life now conjured him instantly to me, a dog made of thought, captured and held by thought, and once in the hands of memory, never let go.

I found myself remembering parts of him through a space too narrow for all to appear at once and still be from him, or else there were only so much recollection and so few memories, and more would not be made: he slept on the couch with his head nearest the bedroom door, he woke me in the morning with bare teeth, for they smile too, many dogs do, and the same happened if I had been away the entire day and he felt the time alone. Whenever he showed his teeth with the gums back, and there was no sound, and the tail was moving, I was being smiled at. How many know? A dog smiles and they hit him for it.

I drove down Main Street and closer to the two shapes beside the police car in the middle of the road, a few cars ahead of me. When it was my turn, one of the policeman flagged me down and I saw it was the same as the man who stopped me on the country road earlier in the day, but the other held him back and waved me on and stared at me as I passed. I saw that it was Troy and I made no move to greet him, knew any gesture would not be returned, was thinking only of the rifle snug in cloth behind the seat. I heard Claire's question again: What are you doing, Julius?

Maybe she had indeed said something to him. But what? What did she know about anything, being gone out of my life a good three years and more? Nothing, that was the sum total of what Claire knew about me.

Passing the last streets of Fort Kent for the open countryside I glanced at the lit front rooms and the people in them. Soon the weather was more on than off. In the late afternoon on the St. John Road a single car came at me in the snow, the headlights growing from a couple of glowing coins to a blinding light splashed over the windshield like water, then the hum of an engine going by, and then nothing, the blue wallpaper of the road and the sky hanging from east to west, the frump of the wipers like a clock. By the time I drove back, the cabin was covered in luminous powder from the clouds.

37

I DECIDED TO KEEP THE CABIN UNLIT AND NOT START a fire either in case they were on their way to surround the place or were already out in the woods with drawn guns. I stood in the dark and gathered my thoughts. After fifteen minutes though all I could feel was the cold, my fingers and knees hurt, and how tempting to throw on a few logs and chase some heat into my joints. I flapped my arms and hopped up and down a few times, twisted my hips. Then I walked to the window and touched the thick web of frost on the pane; my finger stuck to the glass a moment until I pulled it off gently. The woodstove was ice cold, the black heart of the kitchen without its flames. True enough for my father: he once said that all the books together served to insulate the house, and I felt them now, stacked up between me and the rawness outside that pressed a giant white silence down from Canada into every crack of the place. The pulp of pages were trees too and protected me as much as the words in them once did.

I stared outside at the flowerbeds and said, Now I'm as cold as you, Hobbes.

In the pitch black I saw my father sit in front of the fire with his socks against the iron and a book in his hand. What else did he hold? His pipe. Where was his pipe? I thought about it and came to the conclusion that if the police were outside the house they'd have knocked on the door by now or made a different type of entrance, more direct, without the announcement. So I lit a match and waited for a shot to blast through the window, if a man was waiting outside for something to aim at. No shot punctured the glass and I felt no hole appear in me. I followed my other hand with the lit match along the closet until it found the wooden box and in it his English pipe. In the trenches of World War One, the man who lit the first cigarette was least in danger, that was the spark that drew attention; the man who took another light from a match was more in danger as the sniper drew the light into the crosshairs, and the third man to light up in a group was the dead man. Three strikes and you're out.

Kneeling on the floor I detached the head and shook out any flakes, then filled the pipe with the English tobacco stored in the same box, then sat back and puffed away in the dark. A bit stale, the smoke, but a strain of pleasure in the moment, that first taste, the smell that makes the thoughts wander, and those two senses brought my father back even stronger. Now I could hear him turn the pages and call me over and show me a good passage and ask me what I thought, and he would listen for a long time as I spoke, nodding his head and saying how wise I was for a young boy. He was kind that way.

An hour passed and the cold flung stones in my fingers and knees and the muscles pulled at the low bones in my spine. Unable to bear the chill a minute longer, I lit the fire and crept out into the clearing for wood, lifting the tarpaulin for some logs. The rising moon switched its own lamp on in the woods.

No-one shot at me while I carried the logs back into the cabin; no-one shot when I opened the wood-stove and lit the paper under them; no-one shot when I boiled some water for tea and sat in the New England chair with the Shakespeare list from between the books; no-one shot when I held the first page to the fire and read the words in the light of the flames under the glowing pipe. The evening had come, and the dark crept along the walls holding its own weapons, chief among them loneliness and silence, and aimed them at me from every corner at once. I tried to get the fire higher with more wood and filled the cabin with smoke, carelessly enough that I had to open the front door and leave it open for the smoke to blow out, swirling into the night along with the warm air. Bad for the books and the lungs, the eyes and the breath. I stood at the door and watched it sweep off and up into the dark. If they were waiting, now was the moment.

I went back inside when most of the smoke was

gone, pulling off my boots to let my socks steam in the heat. I was my father all of a sudden, isn't that the way it happens. I reviewed a list in the glow: There was a D word, *decipher*, meaning to detect, and a couple of E words: *exhale*, to draw a sword, and *expedient*, fast on one's feet. I smelled the ink again that I wrote them in, now the best part of forty years old, felt the texture of the page and my father's gaze as I curled the letters, felt the comfort of his companionship like gauze wrapped around me.

38

Of my father's death I remember that it was measured like cups he took into himself of a substance designed to end him, accepted with grace and without complaint. His breath had come shallow for a good year, and the distances between objects in the house, the steps from the bathroom to the chair, from the chair to his bed, grew longer and longer for him. It was good that he was a reading man, since that activity required no extra breathing, and for large portions of the day no-one would have known that his lungs were eaten away from the tobacco, except mornings and evenings that passed in coughing, when he turned himself inside out with it, mostly in the final months.

In Fort Kent, the doctor was careful in how he listened to the chest and the lungs, and always shook his head when I spoke to him as my father waited in the car outside. That was our way—the doctor told me his findings, and I informed my father, who was not a man given to doctor visits, and that was the only way I could get him to visit one: I received the message, I made the translation. Most of the time the doctor said that he should stop smoking the pipe, and I would translate it as, You have to cut down on the smoking.

On the last visit, I got into the car where my father waited.

Well? he said.

The doctor says you will be dead in a month. There was no translating that.

He nodded, Well that's to be expected. Don't worry, Julius. You have the house and all those books to take care of.

I drove him home in silence. I wondered if my mother was waiting for him, and if so, where, and if the man I knew was the same one she knew, and how I had never asked him what parts of me were from my mother and what parts were his. Such is what went through my mind as I drove him home in silence.

Three weeks later he took to staying in the chair, and I put blankets round it with a pillow near the head, kept the fire going even though it was April. He slept there too, and I placed some logs on the floor for a footstool. His breath grew louder by the hour and I felt a chill cover him for two days. He stopped speaking then. I saw the pupils in his eyes narrow and knew that he could see me, that I was in his eyes still. I walked my reflection across his eyes, back and forth with logs to the fire and such, to give him the comfort that I was there and not leaving. His voice came back on the third day, and he asked for a Shakespeare, like ordering from a menu at a restaurant, and I waited by the shelves while he chose one.

I'll take the poems, he said, as I watched the back of his head.

I had the book to him in no time, *Collected Sonnets*, 1843 edition, London. Next thing he was reading out loud in a singing voice marking the stresses:

> *That time of year thou mays't in me behold,*
> *When yellow leaves, or none, or few, do hang*
> *Upon those boughs which shake against the cold.*

He had stopped after the word hang in his frail voice and waited a moment till he fell to reading the next line. I walked around in front of him. He looked up at me and smiled. I held his gaze and after a while saw that his pupils observed nothing, no more light affected them, I was nowhere in him, from now on, only in myself. Nothing to tell him anymore, to say how well I'd done with this or that.

Men came from far away, by train and car, by foot the last part, the distance to the plot, and they stood to attention for this man who served with them. The small church in Fort Kent had rarely seen so many corporals and sergeants and privates ranked equally around a grave. I saw battles in their eyes long forgotten by many, and never known to some, and observed some of them fall with him into that hole in the ground, I mean the part of them that remembered the fear and the rubble of distant towns, or the part that had hoped for better things afterwards. The soldier who fights always hopes that way, my grandfather said, but it's those who don't fight who get to decide what things will come. From that day until Claire came out of the woods all those years later, I managed to live on my own, maybe from habit, maybe to honor him. I learned the shape of loss, it was not a stranger to me, since every corner and bench in Fort Kent reminded me of my father, all the places he went. How many times did I pass his grave on my way to buying milk and bread—especially in those weeks after he was first gone, this man of my first thirty years—and wonder how such learning and experience could be switched off like a light.

I sat in the dark and thought such things that would keep me still, perhaps for my safety, a small trick of nature to protect Julius Winsome.

The fire was well lit and still no shot through the window, though Friday night did feel long because I was listening for phantoms in those woods and half dreaming of Claire, probably because I had seen her twice in a short time, but the dreams and the listening swapped places frequently as I sat in the chair between both, sometimes dreaming that Claire was listening, sometimes watching her with a gun in her hand in the woods, watching me, waiting for me to walk outside the cabin. She shoots, I hold a book to my chest, the bullet sinks into the words and stops before my heart.

I was done with shooting.

39

ONLY WHEN I WOKE NEXT MORNING IN THE CHAIR DID I know that I had slept the night before. The last few hours before dawn in deep sleep and without a cover had left me sore. I walked stiffly along the shelves of books, the dark corridor. I clapped my hands to get warm. Water for tea, the fire, more logs from the woodpile, and no footprints in the clearing, that was good. A fine crisp Saturday morning, sky blue, some cloud galvanized along a light wind, a calm before the freeze and on the day before the festival. In Fort Kent the children of the town would be bouncing out of bed and rushing to the window, seeing the same sky, same cloud. Then they run to their parents and remind them that the scarecrow festival is the next day. In seven weeks they will wake and check the pine tree on the night before Christmas, that it was still there and lit and ready for the night, and that there was space enough underneath for the night visitor who was perhaps already a speck above the continents, the eternal father holding the reins, knowing each and every chimney, and each and every name of all children. I wished them all the joy they could hold, every last one, and that he'd leave something for them. If I had a child he would be a reader of course, with all the books; still a child needs friends, even on weekends, and that would mean we'd drive to town a lot, but there was the diner for me to wait in. Such thoughts kept me warm that morning until the fire took hold.

I lit my father's pipe and poured a glass of sherry from the closet into a crystal glass, the one we kept for special occasions. I walked then along the shelves, wondering which book to pick for reading today: the decision was easy in the end, why not? I pulled out Charles Dickens' *A Christmas Carol*. Seven weeks too early but that's why you read ahead, to get into the spirit. And perhaps there was to be a visitor for me soon, a man with a question, a man with a gun. Then I should be outside surely.

From the bedroom I dragged a blanket after me, and walking outside with the sherry on the tray of the book, I threw the bed blanket across a rock out by Hobbes and drank the glass and read for a bit, an hour or so, to give him the feeling he once had with me. It was fairly cold all the same, and eventually I went inside, missing my friend with every step. But a lightness had entered my mind, perhaps leaked gently into it through the long night before, a suggestion that he was at peace now, and that I should be. I was ready for such peace and silence again.

Not fifteen minutes later, deep in the New England chair on a Saturday mid-morning with my second sherry in hand and thirty-eight pages into Dickens, a bullet punctured the woods.

40

SOME PEOPLE WILL SHOOT ANYTHING, ANYTHING IN the world that moves, anything that flies, crawls or swims, anything of the living, furry, feathered, large, small, plump or scrawny, a grouse, woodcock, turkey, pheasant, white-tailed deer, black bear, moose, mice, rats, voles, rabbit, beaver, lynx, bobcat, raccoon, eastern coyote, muskrat, squirrel, otter, fox, mink, weasel, skunk, porcupine, they will do it on fine days, their favorite, on wet days, on days neither fine nor wet, though hunters love the chill in the air, the dank perfume of bark, the forest floor violets, the deer wandering the lakeshore in fog, it all triggers some deep delight in their blood, and if it makes them happy, then so be it, but my father often complained when the shots came five or six to a minute, saying it was hard to be reading in the middle of a broadside. We never heard the shriek of an animal, and that was at least something, but one day my father put down his book and paced the living room, hands behind him, his back slightly bent, his eyes a step ahead of his shoes on the floor.

He said, A battle sniper waits motionless for three hours for a second's aim at a target that will shoot back or call artillery down upon him if he misses. These people out there, and he pointed out the window without looking, they shoot at targets taking a predicable course and without a return shot: you don't have to worry about giving away your position, the flash of the gun muzzle, the steam off the barrel. The worst thing that can happen is you miss or hit but not fatally and they'll go bleeding to find their young.

That was a lot for my father. Then he sat down and found his page again, but too late, I had heard what those shots had loosed in him. That night I dreamed of a feathery archer bending his bow to a nightingale in the branches of a cypress tree.

As a young boy of twelve or thirteen I often took walks in the woods around, though my father explained the places I could not go. One day off a trail forbidden to me I found rusted iron jaws chained to a tree and snapped shut on a leg. To the right in sunlit brush a mountain cat lay on its side. I clung to a tree in fright before seeing flies circle in the sunlight over the stump, a missing front leg. I ran home in tears. My father explained the mystery: the animal had stepped on a hidden hunter's trap, and it chewed first through its own flesh and tendons, then the bone, and tore free. Those who did not, he said, pulled for a few days until hunger outpaced the pain, the string of convulsions, strange sights from the starvation, until they arrived at death and were calmed. He said that the cat's ordeal was over. To the question I did not ask he added that some men must create pain in others to feel less of it themselves.

I soon came to a point in life when I watched for people who came too close to the cabin and the animals we kept. I was twenty or so when I saw a man with a 12-guage looped from his shoulder standing by the pond looking for something to shoot. We had a pet water fowl called Cinder who sometimes went down there, she'd lived on the farm for four years and her mate was somewhere about rummaging in the water basin to clean himself. I heard them calling to each other across the farm a few minutes before. So I stood at the treeline and watched this man. He looked forlorn, balding at the crown, with a tube in the middle, a flannel shirt rolled up and rough at the arms, staring still and silently at an empty pond ringed with plants. Maybe she was in there, he'd spy her and shoot, and she would not survive the blast of pellets. I made a movement and he looked up to me. I did not acknowledge him. He muttered and walked to his left along the pond and into the trees. I put water on for tea and waited for him to come back, since I suspected he was not to be happy that particular day unless he put an end to something. But I was wrong: that man did not return.

It seemed to me that the world and the people abroad in it would not be told where not to go. In summer I had a ring of flowers to stop the forest, in winter a ring of books to stop the cold, to retreat inside for the months of silence. And around me another living ring, the animals that grouped around because of the food I threw down, the birds that hoped for seed in winter and sang their hearts out in spring in return. They lived in a circle of maybe a hundred yards, and in the end they gave their bodies up in peace. I'd find a bird lying in the woods, a mouse curled up by a rock. I hoped I could die so well. Perhaps it is all instinct, men say this. But try stopping a man from doing what he wants: people will not be controlled, they will not be dissuaded, they are also chained to what is in their minds to do, that too might be called instinct. It whips us all.

I tried to read more, but another theme had inserted itself into my thinking. Mine was a minor life, no church steeple scratching at the clouds or joined to the streets of a town, no birthdays and weddings and weekends, a few flowers holding back the forest, a certain number of ducks and guinea hens crackling up in the branches at night. A life all of my own choosing. That thought brought me back to Hobbes, but I had never left him, nor he me. His loss scratched my stomach like burlap, my companion of those years, none to visit him where he lay with his small life, none to know what he was. And now these insistent shots, these reminders.

In the hour that followed, the gunfire came thick and heavy across the yard, the book in my hands. From the sound and the spacing I figured there were two shooters nearby, well within a mile, and whenever I lost myself in the novel, a pair of shots startled the words away brought me back, until my mind left the book altogether and returned to rifles. It became obvious to me that I may not have dealt with the hunter who shot Hobbes after all, that he might still be at large in the area.

Of the shots that banged relentless out of the trees, and closer now too in the last few minutes, one of the two had a familiar ring to it. Something stirred in me again, this deep measure that had the better of me. People were incapable of minding their own business, all this infernal noise they brought with them everywhere.

I feared suddenly that I had reached a time where life had taught me all it was going to or wanted to. From this point on it would be a circle for me, always the same again, and harder to bear at each turn of the wheel when it came round. If I had a child, or someone, I could have led them to what I'd seen and heard over the years, but that was not to be. Around and around, the life of Julius Winsome, day in and out.

I was being shot out of my father's books.

Every year, more and more hunters, better equipped, venturing farther into property, not content to go home without taking something. And if I could not read with all this firing going on, then why have books? The idea caught hold of me, and perhaps because I had not eaten yet or the sherry had gripped my blood or because of the feeling in the air of an approach of some kind, a visitor either of weather or man I don't know, but I imagined myself going inside the house, grabbing a foot-length of books, as many as I could carry in one go, and bringing them out to the clearing and setting them in a stack at the edge of the flowerbeds. And again for the second foot of books, a stack every yard till I had a line of them stretched along the boundary with the forest. What use were books now.

If I did that, it would be best to burn them, not leave them for others, but no big blaze either with smoke everywhere, because in no time I'd have people running with buckets and good intentions, sirens tearing up the road. If I wanted attention, no better way to signal my name in the air than with a smoke blanket. More effective would be one small and secret burning, and then another and another, piles of incendiary words, until the entire library was gone without fuss or notice. Don Quixote? A man my father said had so much information in his head it conjured his mind outside of him. The Parliament of Fowles? Such grace was long gone, long of little use.

But lighting a fire with them was also useless. The cold flakes would wrap themselves around any small flame and snuff it out, and I wondered if I was the complete fool now if I thought I could burn the hours of my childhood and most of my life on a whim or because men had taken to shooting on a morning in early winter.

There would be no transportation of books. I should be dealing with those guns instead.

41

I WALKED INSIDE AGAIN, BRINGING OUT A THIRD GLASS of sherry and sitting by the flowerbed where a few feet down my companion lay wrapped and packed in clay.

He had gone to ground, and ground was in his name: terrier, from the Latin, always digging after quarry. No matter, I could have set a baby down in the clearing in the forest and the pit-bull terrier that was Hobbes would defend that baby from bears, from mountain lions, from anything abroad in that forest, human or otherwise, because it was his job to defend it, even with his own life. And you don't have to starve them and chain them up to make them tough, it's built in, they come out tough. I had treated him like a baby, that's true, and plenty of people will object to that, treating an animal like a human when there's so many hungry people around, why not feed the people first who need feeding. I was sure they fed those hungry people themselves when they got the chance: I didn't know these things. Good luck to them. They could live in their world as long as they stayed out of mine. The trouble with people like that is they can't stay in their own world. And two of them had now evidently strayed where they didn't belong. I rose and walked to the edge of the woods and said to the woods in general,

There's fresh snow fallen, can't you hold off?

I ignored them as best I could for another couple of hours. I read the lists of Shakespeare, from F, *Firstling* and *Flanker*, to G, *Garboil*, *Geck*, *Gallowglass*, *Gallimaufry*, and *Gulf*. I liked the Gs then. But still the shots continued, the two of them and the ammunition that could have sustained a company of soldiers.

My thoughts, it is true, had turned black, the color of Hobbes' world, turned it fast. I could not enjoy the writing and put the list away, walked to the barn and placed the sherry on the bench and lifted the Enfield out of its case, set it across my shoulder with a fresh clip in the magazine. I saw another clip handy on the bench and wanted to carry it too, but it would drag in my pocket, so I left it behind me. I also left the telescopic sight behind.

I took the white blanket off Hobbes' grave and draped it on my other shoulder over the long coat and set off into the woods toward the sound of the shots. It was easy to follow them, they came regular, a couple a minute. Those men must have brought a garrison's worth of cartridges with them. What were they hunting, the entire northern herds? Were they not aware that it was one deer per person per season? These I could tell were heavy-caliber rifles, auto-repeaters, also illegal for hunting as far as I knew. Well-armed men, shooting well and careless as to the law. Could easily have been one of those two then who had done the shooting. It was even likely, if that man weren't dead already.

42

TWENTY MINUTES INTO THE WOODS AND IN THE GENTLY
falling flakes I came silently upon a man. He was wearing orange and made no attempt to disguise himself.

I had not heard anything for five minutes and then there was this crack of fire in the middle distance: he stood in his orange huntsman's vest, shooting rapidly at two deer feeding in the adjacent field. Another minute and I would have stumbled on top of him had he been quiet enough, or stumbled down dead if he had been waiting for me.

I unslung the rifle and watched him. One of the deer crumpled at the rear, he had caught it in the hind leg. The deer looked ahead to where the other ran, trying to follow, to gain a foothold on the flat grass. The hunter shot again, this time splashing a bullet into the neck and flattening the deer motionless on its right side.

I waited for another minute. The huntsman did not move from his firing position, did not walk to check on the shot, which I thought strange. Perhaps he was waiting for the mate to return to shoot it too, but he knew surely that the deer would not return, not that soon. Now where was the other shooter? Had I mistaken the sound of one rifle for two? Was he alone?

I heard myself whisper, perhaps too loudly: By your shots I deciphered two of you, and each with his rifle exhaled, expedient back and forth in the woodland.

Yes, I did count two rifles. The other must have been off hiding or tracking another animal. I waited for another couple of minutes and then eased up the safety and gently pulled the bolt, and then I looked up to aim as I raised the rifle, and I saw the man's gun pointed at me, and he looked panicked. I stepped to the left as his finger pulled the trigger, that same instant, and the bullet smacked the bark of the tree at my right ear, scoured a foot of bark that shredded itself onto my shoulder and into my eye. He should not miss the second time, not at this range, even in a panic. I moved back to the right and brought the rifle up. I breathed in and he shot again, and some god-awful fire ran the skin of my left shoulder; I aimed with my good eye and breathed out and pulled the trigger, and his head cracked around the hole and he fell like carrots from a torn bag, dead a long time before he hit the ground.

I pulled back the bolt handle and checked the wound: superficial, nothing that would bleed much. My father had taught me well. Never hurry a shot. This man could have had me if he had waited a tenth of a second. He may have been expecting me: his shooting might have been bait to draw me out. But that was brave of him to stand out like that and shoot in an orange top. And why kill the deer? But why kill a dog? And foolish of him in the end, surely, though you don't want to be mocking the dead.

It was a good thing I didn't budge, because a truck ripped through the saplings and tore the foliage as it made for me, a big half-ton with blue paneling and tinted glass. A pump gun hung out the driver's side window and sprayed shot pellets with the first report, and the second sound I focused on was the driver sliding the pump action. Must have been turning the steering wheel with his knees, most likely. I ducked as the shot sliced the undergrowth around my feet and a hot knife stabbed my knee.

I slowed the truck down in my mind: he was six, seven seconds from me, and if I ran he would drive over me within a few steps, there were so few large trees in this spot. I remembered the position of the grille and tracked the trajectory by its chrome, brought the rifle up and aimed three feet and seventy degrees from the front corner and fired. The cartridge splintered the windshield a hand wide and entered his right eyebrow. His head flicked to his left and he stared out the window as the truck locked in a circle and slammed against a tree, trying to mount it as the tires spun.

I did not move, a frozen man in his white blanket. I would not make that mistake twice. The engine of the truck ran high: the driver's foot must have jammed against the pedal. The woods were so quiet, the truck so loud. As if another person beside me performed the action, the bolt slid and another round went into the firing chamber.

I had three bullets to my name.

I stayed low and watched, breathing the relief. I was lucky with the speed of reloading: the bolt handle on a Lee Enfield is set back behind the trigger, which makes chambering smooth and fast, twelve shots a minute. My grandfather said that when the Germans first faced the British infantry lines equipped with Enfields, they thought they were under machine gun fire. The bolt action, the engineering of the thing, had saved me.

I decided to check the truck, now that both men were down, and placed the rifle on the snow and moved to the passenger side window, the white blanket covering my head. He was still alive, and I recognized him. It was Pascal, the complaining man from outside the supermarket, the one with the gun, the law and order man. By way of comfort I said something to him from Hunt magazine, something a hunter would understand:

I honor your sacred spirit, and the firstling too, your friend. But I had to take you.

I'll kill you, he whispered, and slumped like a man snoozing. I must have seemed like a ghost to him, a spirit come to take him away. Some men won't go quietly.

They say you glimpse the bullet that will kill you.

I am sure I saw this one. It came from his side of the truck, through his side window, passed in front of his face and along my right temple and whipped the saplings behind me like a spit.

A third man.

43

THE SNIPE IS A SHOREBIRD, A FAST WADER IN MARSH ground with a long, slender bill that sews for insects and such. When it sees you it crouches until the last moment and then bursts out of the grass, flying crookedly, an impossible dart through the air. A long time ago some men were fast enough with a rifle to put an aim on one and shoot it out of the sky. Those men went sniping.

Sniper. The word drifted across the trenches in 1914 and became a soldier's word: a hidden man who made people disappear one at a time, a man who knew camouflage and wore the countryside on top of him, whether crouched or crawling, selecting a position, or observing the stir of a hand at a hundred yards and putting a shot through it. If captured he could expect little other than be executed like a spy, because his uniform was the invisible, because his eye looked along the sight and made entire platoons take cover, because he killed people's friends. There must be something missing in him, an empathy gone or never there to begin with, so he receives none in return.

These days, from what I'd heard recently, anyone who lifted a rifle was called a sniper, when most likely it was just an angry man or a cruel boy with a powerful weapon on a clock tower or in a bush along the highway, shooting innocents because they happened to be there. Sniper: the very word is quickly said, but the best of them are slow, patient, deliberate men. I had heard that word on the open street in town the day before, heard discussion of a possible shooter who had lately killed some hunters, for what else could have happened to these men, gone off and left their families? No such thing. And when I went for groceries, the word was that they were definitely missing, these men, and it was clear to me that the people in the supermarket were giving themselves up completely to rumors and talk of rumors. The authorities were searching now, but that is the nature of hunting, that shots are fired in the wilderness. Anyway, I knew myself as no sharpshooter, lacking the training and true patience required. They must have been discussing another individual, though it is true that I was involved in a few incidents recently.

They say it takes an unbalanced mind to hold a rifle that steady. But my father said the English sniper who gave my grandfather the Pattern 14 Enfield was a happy man who said he was glad to see the end of the fighting and wanted to spend the rest of his life in a small country town with a church spire and the tinkle of bells in the evening, the rustle of sheep and the warm smell of the sea in summer. Of this reputed imbalance in the heads or minds of marksmen my father said little, other than that the best sniper is passionate and cold at the same time, awkward up close, best at a distance.

That sounded like balance. I hoped this third man was not of that kind. If so I was breathing the last of this life into me already.

44

I THOUGHT I SAW A FACE AT TWO HUNDRED YARDS, AND
I ran from the truck to my rifle and dove to the ground,
hooking the Enfield in my left hand and sliding to a
halt while holding the blanket above me with my right,
to cover my hair.

To my right I heard the truck still trying to strad-
dle the tree—that noise could be my undoing—no way
to track the sniper, to gauge his shooting. That blasted
truck. The trigger of the rifle was five inches forward of
my hand. No, this was the thing, not to move. I lay
under the blanket and breathed face down, deep and
slow. A shot punched the snow a yard to my left, another then two yards to the right, judging by the shiver and
puff. He was trying pot luck. Good: he could not see
me. That meant he didn't have a telescopic sight or
wasn't willing to sacrifice his wide but poor view for a
better one and possible exposure. He should have.
Another shot, this one inches from my skull. Maybe he
did see me but aimed poorly.

I kept my face in the snow. The chill petrified my

bones and lips. Not to show my face, this took some restraint as my mind kept imagining him sneaking up on me and all I had to do to save my life was look up and see him stalking. Now he stands over the blanket and aims down on me. Look up, Julius. Look up! But I knew that if I looked up I would distinguish myself from the snow with my pink face and die. I felt my heart palpitate, a tremor cordis in me.

I had time to kill, so I whispered to the snow the two words under F that I had read before leaving for the woods. I could not bring to mind a third, something of no use, it must have been.

Then I slid back the first inch and waited.

No shot came.

Then I moved another inch, this time to my right, toward the truck. No shot. At two hundred yards, the eye cannot catch an inch of movement at a time, a foot, definitely, but not the tiny inch. For thirty minutes after that I moved but one inch at a time, with ten seconds' rest between each inch, a World War One battle maneuver against an active sniper, a story told by my grandfather to my father and so to me. It still worked. Not long now. I knew I was safe when I felt the truck's tires spin at my ear. I held up a pinch of the blanket and glanced sideways. Yes. The truck was now between me and the rifleman: I had covered fifteen feet. He was cautious, too cautious for a hunter. I rolled to one side and brought the rifle to my chest, moved the bolt and chambered a new round. He heard it somehow through that damned engine, and a bullet ripped the snow where my head had lain thirty minutes before.

For him to shoot now was surely foolish: he had given away his position for no reason. Better to have remained silent and alert. Sooner or later I would have had to rise and he would see me, or night would fall and we could both have gone home.

I rolled a yard to the right and held the blanket out before me, waited, then moved my head under it, nudging at the flap with a finger one quarter inch and inserted my eye into that space.

I found him where I saw him first, and clear as daylight. He had made a crucial mistake: he forgot about his boots. He had worn a white top and scarf for his head, good camouflage, but when a man lies prone in the snow, the heels of his boots are at a higher elevation than his head, about two inches, and his boots were black. You have to paint the heels of your boots the color of the landscape if you want to lie down with your rifle. And there they waved like two black flags. By aiming right between the boots and down a fraction, I had a headshot.

Three bullets. How confident was I? The truth was my hands and face were numb from lying in the snow. I could not trust the aim and had to go around him. I don't know how much time I spent closing the distance, though it was easier with the trees as cover. I can say that about one hour after he fired upon me, I brought my rifle to my shoulder at a distance of ten yards from him, off to his side.

Something told him. He looked and saw me.

This man's face in front of me now was cleaned away with fear, but the traces left on it told me all I needed to know.

45

I RECOGNIZED HIM, WHICH IS TO SAY THAT I DID NOT shoot him dead on the spot, this man who had sent three or four cartridges my way, any one of which would have crumpled my frame like a wet egg under my blanket and coat. He turned on his side and arched his rifle over his head, but I had the barrel centered between his eyes and he looked at me straight down along the sights and let it fall, still holding it, into a depression at his side, a place he should have put himself in to begin with, his body lower than his rifle.

It's you, he said. I knew it was you.

I said, If you knew it, you didn't take advantage.

I brought the aim to his chest so I wouldn't miss if he moved. So we're on speaking terms after all, I said.

Shooting me will be different.

Really, I said. I don't think so. I shoot you, you die. It'll be the same, I think, that's the truth of it.

I mean shooting a police officer.

No, It'll still be the same for you, I said. And as for

what happens to me, you needn't worry about that. You won't worry.

He seemed to have exhausted his store of words, so I spoke again for him.

And I'm surprised to hear you say anything to me, I said.

He eyed his rifle, brazen as could be. As if I was just going to stand there.

I have a question, I said, using my shoulder to wedge the rifle while I fished the drawing out of my pocket half way before stuffing it back suddenly. Didn't want to be fiddling with paper now. He'd have that thing up in a flash.

Did you shoot my dog, I said. It was around here, as a matter of fact, that he was shot, this close to my home.

I did not, he said. Is this what this is all about, a dog?

I brought the rifle up. Your final words on the matter?

Then he broke all at once like a china cup on a concrete floor, his hands covering his face, as if they'd stop a .303 shell. A loud shriek. Jesus, please don't kill me. Please. I don't want to die.

Troy, I said, keeping the rifle at eye level while risking the familiar first name, I'm far from being Jesus these days.

I won't tell anyone. No, no dog shooting, it wasn't me.

He grabbed for his weapon and I kicked it away, shot at the ground in front of him as he lunged after it and re-chambered while he jerked from the shock, scrabbling around in the snow and around himself for bullets, grabbing away at nothing in his clothes, no holes, no blood. He looked up at the rifle and flinched as it went back to him. He covered his head and waited for it.

What line of business are you in, I said, aiming.

He screamed, then realized I had spoken and not shot.

He said, You know. His voice shook like a pond under a breeze.

I don't mean your job. I heard once you have a business on the side, evenings possibly.

Security, he said. I own a security firm.

Security, I said.

He nodded.

Is it a success?

He nodded.

I said nothing then. The truck engine was tiresome and I wanted to switch it off, was tired of speaking loudly over it, this dead man over there riding his truck.

It is true that frightened men urinate. The body ditches everything for flight. Troy's pants ran.

I said, Take off your jacket.

He pulled off the white jacket. I told him to empty the pockets and saw a phone and keys and such fall out. He stood in a flannel shirt, black, with beige at the collar.

What time is it? I said.

He looked at his wrist. After four.

Now we'll go home, I said. Put it back on, and turn your friend's key for him.

Wondering what the trick was, when and where the bullet would tear into him, he scrambled up and got into the jacket before pulling the white scarf off his whiter neck. After he turned his confederate's truck off, he had another question for me.

Where's home? he said.

Second star to the right, I said.

What?

Follow me but by being in front. Home is ahead, and no more banter from you.

We walked back to the cabin under the rising moon and the faint glow of snow, two men and their footsteps, one holding a rifle to the other's back, the oldest arrangement of power.

46

I WAS IN NO HURRY TO SAY ANYTHING, ONLY TO REACH the house before complete darkness. That was some garboil in the woods, I said.

I don't understand, he said.

I meant disorder in the woods. You and your distraction of gallowglass.

Gallows?

The loose infantry of all of you in there, I said.

We passed the heavier trees, the deep middle woods.

You must have taken me for a right geck with that truck blasting through the woods at me, I said. Did you think I would run and then you shoot me?

That was the plan, he said.

You were with them, then. You were the flanker.

We came together. I was to wait for the shot, the truck was to shake you out of the woods.

And the first man?

What's a geck, he said.

A fool. The first man?

He didn't know that we were out to trap you and believed we were hunting for the afternoon. Told him he could shoot all the deer he wanted to because I'm the law. He was the decoy. I thought we would have you before you shot. Yes, I was on the flank.

You see, you understand if you listen, I said. And you should have told him your plan and not let him stand alone. That could be construed as reckless in some quarters.

We walked then in silence for twenty minutes until I saw the porch light gleam through the gallimaufry of trees—every sort of tree—if I'd been explaining things to him. I was happy to be at the cabin, tired of this man and his urgency, his importance.

Stand over there, I said, and he walked to the flowerbed, looking around him, checking for an out, a dash into the woods, the place in the play that says Exeunt. A good place for him to leave the stage, I thought, there beside Hobbes, Hobbes the groundling.

Would you like a sherry, I said, standing in the doorway. I could see him itching to run, wondering whether I'd miss, knowing I would not.

I don't drink, he said.

Fair enough. What time is it?

He looked: Five.

I kept the rifle on him. Now tell me you did not shoot the dog.

I had nothing to do with it.

Say it again.

I did not shoot the dog. It ran at me along the trail but was only barking at me.

Tiredness and stress must have brought him off his guard. I saw the turmoil in him as he tried to take back what he'd just said. A policeman should know more than to open his mouth unless he knows what's coming out of it. All the men who march themselves off to prison with their own mouths.

What do you mean, I said, that he was only barking?

He pursed his lips, sullen, and lifted low and murderous eyes to me that met the Enfield staring back.

Answer me that question, I said. Answer it now.

47

If a man whispers something to you in German, and you don't speak that language, you won't understand a word of it: he could be talking philosophy or cursing your parents. If he shouts the same thing or different German words at you, you still won't understand a thing. When a dog lifts his head and howls while keeping his eyes on you, slightly from the side, it means he's playful but knows you're putting one over on him. If he puts his head back and barks at you full on, down from the stomach, he wants to play. If he growls from the stomach when you grab him and looks sideways at you, it's pure affection, but if he growls straight ahead and shallow from the teeth, it's a one-second warning. If you don't understand his language, it's all noise. Those men abroad in the woods did not, I think, understand my Shakespeare, though every word of it was English and I spoke carefully. I may as well have been barking at them. Time makes dogs of us.

48

IT WAS ALMOST DARK, AND TROY STOOD WHERE THE flowers had perfumed the entire clearing and my bedroom in the mornings, he stood where the light of the porch reached now to cover us.

He said, It was another time, over a year ago. I came up here to the woods, to see where you lived. I was tired of Claire talking about you; she had mentioned your name twice in four years, and so I had to see what was going on, to understand the competition I was dealing with. I walked along the woods out there meaning to check out the cabin, and your dog heard me, ran through the woods at me. I got into the truck and drove away.

You said he was barking.

He barked, that's all he did. Why would a man shoot a barking dog?

I lowered the rifle. So Hobbes had stood his ground. Either that or this was an incident with the dog that this man had time to fancy up on the long silent walk back. No, maybe poor Hobbes was competition for Troy too, had she really talked about Hobbes to him? I thought I asked out loud, but Troy did not move to speak.

Then, as a white flurry blended through the trees and the last leaves tore from the branches, I remembered Claire wearing no clothes and standing in the warm kitchen a few weeks after her first visit, holding a copy of *The Winter's Tale* to her breast.

> *Here's flowers for you;*
> *Hot lavender, mints, savoury, marjoram;*
> *The marigold, that goes to bed with the sun*
> *And with him rises weeping: these are flowers*
> *Of middle summer, and I think they are given*
> *To men of middle age.*

You are my own William now, she said to me.

I found myself looking at the place where the flowers appeared, those which I had grown myself or that grew by themselves, pressing themselves above the hard ground for light.

Such soft skin, such a hard memory.

Troy stood at the flowerbed, sulking. Then a murder of crows, thousands of them, a rattle of black, flew mid way up through the trees, a trickling shrill band. They took five minutes to pass, and the noise ruled out any words between us in the meantime. Troy watched the rifle, and I watched the birds pass behind him.

The trees are crowed, I said.

He winced. They're what? What are you saying?

That word was of my own making, I said. My Shakespeare has run out for the moment.

His sullen shrug, as if we had parted languages and he was staying behind. Defiancy, another new word, just for him. But I admired his focus, the strength and purpose of his will: he thought in a way that excluded everything from it that did not fit in, the way a moth stitches itself to the light bulb on the porch, a knitting circle, and sometimes its shadow bothered me and I switched off the light to free it into the night, since only silence sends people like Troy away, since if you say anything they must at once attach a reply.

Do you want to come in, I said. The evening was settling in.

He shook his head, eyes drifting to the cabin. I'm not going in there.

As you like, I said. But they'll be going down badly soon, the numbers.

He must have thought I was talking about something else because he said, And you've shot a good number of people already, haven't you?

I took a drink, the temperature was mixing the sherry differently on my tongue. I nodded to give him that victory, since he deserved it:

I said, There's an idea abroad that men with guns can do as they wish, that it's the natural order of things. I gave them a natural order.

So you admit it, here and now, he said.

He was warming up to his plan to survive, whatever that was. I was past the point where it mattered to me, about myself, about anything. All I felt was an absence that had never been there before, that blanketed everything in me. Before this I knew the normal happiness in being alone disturbed suddenly by one absence: the sheer hardness of it, you become a stone, a wood, a splinter in the ground, wind with splinters in it. And as poisonous remedy, the flowers in all the grey, the touch of a hand on your arm, the sweet word from a smile, what cures and then leaves you worse. Some people think it is the mind that does it. If that were the case, whether Hobbes had ever been in my life, or I in his, mattered little to the world or anyone in it, only to me now. You attach yourself and suffer when you don't have it anymore. But he made my days shorter when I had no one else, his friendship present even when no gain occurred.

And you can admit something for me now, I said.

I spoke deliberately, sure that I was speaking out loud and not to myself since living as I did sometimes blurred the two.

Troy moved his legs to shoulder width. Admit what?

That you sent a man out yesterday to check on me, the man on the road in the morning. I saw two men in the car afterwards.

Troy began nodding before I was done. I sent a man out, dropped him off and picked him up after you drove through. You have some eyesight, I'll give you that, he said.

But you didn't follow me, I said.

You would have seen us. But I had a rifle on you the whole time he was questioning you.

And now, I said, you are here today, you came with these men to the woods, neither of them a constable, and both of them working for you it seems, to get me out looking for you.

Only one of them knew, not the first you killed. Anyway, I figured I could get you myself before any shooting started.

And be the hero.

Just doing my job.

I doubt that, I said. Doing your job would not have had you employing another man to die today. I incarnadined your intelligencer.

My Shakespeare had returned but skipped the H words. He seemed puzzled, so I translated the English into English: I bloodied your spy.

That set him off.

You're mad because I took Claire away from you, he said. That's it, that's what this is all about, isn't it? Not some damn dog.

I could see the fear and defiance again stir in him like milk into tea. And when I arrived at his curse as I reviewed the order of his words, the curse placed before Hobbes, my blood went low in my body, down in cold parts under the veins. Claire was, I had to believe, as distant from all of this as could be, and bringing her into it was ill-advised on his part. But I owed him the respect of following his own logic:

If that were so, if you are the instigator of everything that has happened, the man whose power I live under, then you would be the man equally to end it all by his death. If I am jealous, I said lifting the rifle, I can remedy that now.

I aimed at his forehead. He grew whiter and faster than snow blizzards a windshield. I could tell he was thinking of running, the way he met my gaze down the barrel without flinching. His training told him to do that, not to betray his thinking with an unconscious glance around him for an escape route. To stare at me instead as if he were intent upon me only. Good for him, to have that resource of mind. I had underestimated him.

I glanced to one side for him, to let him know.

Unless you can become a tree I wouldn't try to run, I said, thinking that he should elect to see the bullet rather than have it travel after him.

He sensed the moment had come and stiffened against the shot he expected. I breathed out.

You wouldn't treat an animal like this, he said. Some pleading now.

Does treat mean well or badly, I said.

You know, he said.

I must know what to do with you then, if that's what you expect from that word. I would have thought treating like an animal meant well.

I brought the rifle back up as I had dropped it an inch to answer him and I wanted that breath to be the last thing he ever heard. A cold blast banged us both hard, a cloud moved off the yellow rising moon. It was all but dark, thirty minutes at most. The forest was showing its white hand, the sky closing its fist.

I heard his next words at the second the trigger was at the pressure of firing.

Claire, he said.

I froze at the sights. What about Claire?

He spoke again, his hands up from his sides: She'll miss me.

What has Claire to do with you and me, I said. Only in your head.

But he sensed the hesitation, and the proof was that he was still alive. He did not waste time, mostly because lately he had less than a second of it to his name.

He said, What about her, her feelings, what will she do?

She'll live, I said.

How? I can give Claire a family, children, a family life. What could you have given her?

That stopped me. It was a good question. I wanted to smoke a Turkish cigarette, drink strong coffee against the falling twilight, what I loved most about the day, that chink in the door. But there was Troy and given a moment he'd snap himself out of my sight.

I said, I don't know anymore. I'm not sure that people give anything to anyone as such.

Well I can give her a family, a sense of values.

I know what those words mean, I said, and let the rifle down. Enflields are heavy, even for a grown man, when you hold them up long enough.

He said, Then you can put those words into practice.

He was being earnest or else an actor in the first league. I had left the sherry on the porch railing, nothing to do but shoot the man or talk to him.

I have an example, I said.

Yes, he said. Go ahead. I'll listen.

I said, The guinea hens go into the bushes and sit on eggs and leave them only when it becomes a matter of life or death. I see the female walk scraggily out of the bush in the evening, and three males walk about her in a triangle protecting her as she goes to the feeding place.

That's a start, he said.

I said, A chicken hawk once darkened the yard and most of the animals ran for the trees except the chickens. And the hawk swooped on one and lifted it. Hobbes was already at full stretch even when the hawk was still on the way down, and he leaped for the chicken in the hawk's talons, jumped well up, and the hawk let go, and Hobbes fell to the ground with the fowl.

Troy had no response for that, as if he had not heard or believed me. But I had seen it happen. The good policeman went to another page in his survivor's manual.

Make it easy on yourself. Give yourself up, he said.

I was disappointed. There you go with your give again.

Make it easy on yourself, he said.

It's already easy on me.

I decided to be silent for a while, to let him make the next move. It chafed at him. He said something but the wind caught it and anyway I wasn't answering him for the moment. And if he moved he was a dead man in that second.

When I was young I heard a visitor to the farm point to the ducks we kept and say to my father that they were being unnaturally protected against predators, that in the real world they fend for themselves, that the laws of nature favor the strong. The sun was shining that day and the ducks were in the water of the upturned basin lid they had crowded into, corded their necks together and slept. My father listened, nodded, offered him more tea, and they talked some more. Then he said,

You don't mind if after you've finished that tea— he pointed to it—that I go inside and get a shotgun and kill you with it?

I don't understand, the man said, shifting in his seat.

Surely you must, my father said. Because I have a shotgun and you don't, I'm stronger than you so I can shoot you, according to your philosophy. His voice had a lilt in it even though the matter was technically a threat, according to the visitor who left shortly after that. The story went around town but it was put down to the war. At the end of the day my father had a rare twinkle: A war can be handy like that, he said. And then, the twinkle gone, he added, You cannot believe in survival of the fittest but want to decide first who is the fittest to survive.

Survival of the fittest, I said.

What? Troy whitened again. I had spoken aloud, spoken myself out of the past, people dead and gone. And that brought me back to the books, the book in my pocket.

Troy followed where I was looking.

A cup of tea would have been a miracle for me, but I knew that a second of lost attention would bring me around to the wrong end of my own rifle and that Troy would shoot me at once, not trusting himself to bring me all the way to the station ahead of him through the woods. He'd be right.

I told him to take the book with the piece of paper I had slipped recently into it and stand at the flowerbeds. He grabbed the book and walked, step by slow step, his eyes flicking from the ground to the gun, judging the moment of a last desperate run he knew he could not finish. Yet that truth has never stopped anyone.

The night was upon us now, with its own strange light, the light of the other side, smaller and in pieces

but enchanting and a salve for those whose lives blos-
som under it. That same light carries voices better. His
had fallen thinner, less confident, or maybe the light
made it seem so:

He said, What did she see in you anyway?

His voice shook with a trace of something that
didn't have metal in the sentences, the way people talk
who believe everything they believe. But perhaps I was
the same myself, had my own cogs driving what I
thought and said, full of my own belief. I was part of it
all, that was for sure.

You'd have to ask her that. She chose you.

He looked down to what he was holding: What is
this?

Read the lines on the paper, I said.

He opened the book to where the paper stuck out
and lifted it, and covered the writing up and down with
a glance, puzzled and panicked to be reading his last tes-
tament, and that not even in his own words.

I said read it.

Okay, okay. He traced the words with a finger,
the finger falling behind his eye, his voice trailing the
finger:

Let's make us medicines of our great revenge,
To cure this deadly grief.

What do you think, I said.

It's a foreign language, I don't understand this
continual talk of yours.

It's English, I said.

What—you mean like intelligencer, and that other word you said? That's not English.

I knew what he was saying and felt for him.

You mean it's English like a dog's bark, I said.

Yeah, that's exactly what I mean, what it's like.

I said, They might be the same thing now.

What's the same?

What dogs and Shakespeare have to say.

Who says? He snapped the book shut and pointed to his chest: What's with this lecturing me? What are you going to do? I'm a police officer.

He shouted these words to give them force, but they were the right words and didn't need shouting. It was true for him, I had far too much to say all of a sudden, a form of impertinence.

I kept the rifle high. My intendment? I don't know, I said by way of a fast retreat. Read a little, make some tea, get a fire going with this chill coming, something along those lines is what I will do.

His voice softer again: I meant do with me.

I shook my head to let him know, and at that he melted for his final moments, they loosened him into talking more, complaints about his life and his business, how hard he had worked, how everyone respected him, and then his lists of responsibilities, and I waited till the complaints echoed themselves into the silence of the forest that eats up everything a man might ever say till he has talked himself out and the echoes peter because no generation follows them into the trees.

I knelt on one knee and wiped off the snow from Hobbes, from the clay above him. He was a couple of feet away from my hand, and I felt I could almost rub his back, pat his head.

Had Troy shot Hobbes? I believe I was leaning that way. His manner when he denied it, the quickness of his explanation, what he knew. He admitted being around the cabin and had the streak required for such an act, to silent what was already voiceless.

I stood with the Enfield, pointed it at his stomach. Tell me she's happy, I said.

He looked surprised and said nothing for a change, maybe because the lights were out in the sky, only stars in the clear night ahead of tomorrow's storm. He thought for a minute or looked at his boots without thinking, I couldn't tell. And that chill at my arms, at my ears. The trees seemed to move differently behind him, surely the numbers on their way, that's what it was, sucking any heat from the air.

Is she happy? I haven't—I think so.

The first uncertainty out of him all day. I looked again at the beds, the width of snow I'd scraped away, a small scrap off the face of death, as useless as digging him up and holding him again. To have him so close and not have him at all.

So she was happy. I knew at those words that she was truly gone and likely never to pass before me again, no woman come out of the woods, no ointment in the air of the cabin, no voice reaching out a hand for mine in the kitchen after nightfall, by the fire. I still loved her, if that's what this feeling was in me, this memory. But there was Hobbes, taken from me, taken from his own life, his joy.

I stood and said, That's good then. You'll need to be on your way.

I glanced to the trees that led to Fort Kent, as if some trees held a highway in them and those were the ones for him to follow.

You're going to kill me, he said.

I said nothing to that, but it was true, I had gone back and forth. He was the one. I had him now.

49

HE LOOKED WHERE I POINTED, AT THOSE TREES, THEN at others around him as if to confuse me or himself as to where he intended to run. He breathed deeper, storing air for the dash.

You're going to shoot me.

I told you to go. How many times do you have to be told something?

I owed Claire that much, to bring this man back to his house and to her. The impulse to let him go needed quick nurturing before a stronger one came back, before my eyes passed over the flowerbeds where Hobbes lay on his side, silent in his end, what waits for everyone.

He stepped to the rear, one foot searching, then the other, facing me, not taking the chance to turn his back and run.

You will do something for me, I said.

He stared.

Never, I said, never on your life say another word to me, and don't look in my direction ever again, unless it's to be your final glance.

He did not wait for further instructions, and I saw that he was walking away from town and my cabin, back into the woods where we met earlier. That meant he had a vehicle parked somewhere near where I found him.

Very presumptuous, I said.

What? He did not move to face me again.

You'll be walking back to Fort Kent, I said, or some of the way. And Fort Kent is that way. I waved the rifle at the invisible town in the other direction. Go on. Forget your car. And cover your gulf.

He did not ask what a gulf was but curled the scarf around his throat anyway and walked across the yard in front of me, this policeman heading off to Fort Kent on foot. When he was twenty yards into the brush, fifty steps distant in the snow, I aimed the rifle at the back of his head, as he no doubt expected me to do, and pulled on the trigger until a finger's tension and release balanced him on this and the far side of life.

Look around, Troy, I said.

He did not. That surprised me. He struck me as the type who has to do what you tell him not to. I thought he would shout something at me then as he flitted along the floor of the woods, walking faster. I would shoot him if he did, pursue him to the very end of him. He ran finally, sifting himself away into the trees, and I loosened the trigger and brought him back to this life, and he was gone, along with my chance of shooting him into the next, gone carrying my last embrace to Claire, this man who took her from me and whose life she had just saved.

There were no houses this side of the first major road, and that was a good three-hour walk in these conditions, at the very least, assuming he didn't get lost. Then he would be picked up, someone would be driving the St. John Road on a Saturday night, and then there was another twelve miles to Fort Kent, so at least five hours until they came this way, more likely after midnight by the time they had all their men and cars and plans, and he with them, of course, to regain his dignity. That was fine. I leaned the rifle on the porch and went inside.

50

First I made tea and got the fire burning high, packed with logs, then did something I could not remember having been done in all the time I had grown up in that cabin: I took the New England chair from its place in front of the woodstove and carried it out to the clearing, set it down in the middle between the porch and the flowerbed, facing the space in the trees where the sky held most of the stars. When I walked back into the cabin I saw the giant space where it had been and the man who sat in it, and all the reading that had passed months and years in it, the stories that turned the pages on that chair.

In the spare bedroom I lifted the cover from the gramophone and placed a record, turning the volume till I knew I'd hear it outside and setting the arm to repeat; all that was left to do was select a book. I walked the shelves to S for Shakespeare, midway between the cold books at the back and the warm ones on the other side of the horseshoe of bookshelves that ended at the kitchen counter. With my coat and gloves with the fingers showing I took it outside to the chair and sipped the tea as the song floated overhead.

Wouldn't be long now, not that long to wait. I leaned back in the chair and watched the stars and guessed from the disposition of cloud that it was snowing in a corner of the woods, yet I hoped that my patch of sky would stay open for another hour. The record played from deep in its scratches the lute and a tender voice from long ago and far away. I closed my eyes and let it drift over me, kept the cup against my fingers for the heat:

> *Greensleeves was all my joy,*
> *Greensleeves was my delight,*
> *Greensleeves was my heart of gold,*
> *And who but my Lady Greensleeves.*

I thought I might as well read for a while, the part of *The Winter's Tale* that she held up to me near the end, the part I thought she must have meant, though she was not the type to read much of anything aloud:

> *A sad tale's best for winter: I have one*
> *Of sprites and goblins.*

I drew the gabardine around me to wrap out the chill, and at that second the page brightened and I knew, looked up, there, sharp and icy in the night, now above the trees and out of the ringing cloud, the white rock spun its stringed music, unheard, above the white lamp of ground and into the black rooms of the air.

Won't be long now.

Soon the cold was upon me, the merciless and nameless cold, and I needed the blanket I'd draped on the porch railing. Walking it back to the chair reminded me of my grandfather, when he lived under that same cloth as now kept me warm and had earlier saved my life: he spent the day long under it by the fire, and when I asked him once what he was thinking, he put his hand on my shoulder and said he was thinking of my mother, as she had died only six few years before, and that he had been fond of her, that I would have liked her, and not to worry about the bits of me that didn't make sense because I never knew her. She was in me, and that was all.

After an hour or so of that tune I was ready for the next. The fire was turning to a mush of red-hot ember as I passed quietly to the bedroom and placed another record on the turntable, songs by John Dowland, a lute player from Shakespeare's time: I saw the first three titles circle on the label: *Flow Not so Fast Ye Fountains, Come from My Window, Flow Now my Teares.*

On the way out I poured hot water for coffee to keep myself awake and carried it on top of a pillow so I could lean back and see the sky without straining. Before I got too comfortable, I went into the barn and spread all the seed, the cracked corn and pellets for the birds, all of it across the floor and into the yard, and wedged the door open so they could get in and out. From the window I heard more scratches and wondered how the sound of the record could reach this far, then saw the bundle of wings unfurl in the light of the moon and the claws scratch the glass, and the small bird flung itself once more at the sky it couldn't reach. You think the moon is the sun, you do, I smiled, and you should be asleep, and I walked to it with my coat spread wide. It scattered itself into the folds, caught as I closed them. Goodness knows how long you've been trying. I carried the soft punch of its feathers into the yard and opened wide, and it flew up and was gone.

Not long now.

I was restless as a man waiting for a performance, an empty hand stretched out too far for another hand, an ear lost between notes. There was only one thing for it, the pipe would calm me, that and another sherry. I stoked the fire first, then poured a glass and lit the pipe, puffing my way out to the clearing.

The wind came and slit me along the skin. This time I knew it for a snow wind, the way the trees rattled like fine silver, the sound of a trembling arctic sea across the tops of the forest. That same wind must have bounced off the trees and brushed the moon too, because when I looked up I saw it bulged slightly on the left side, like water in the thinnest reach of the wave when it spreads and then seeps, a bright salt stain on the sand.

My father's astronomy book was correct to the

hour in predicting the event to come, what he pointed out to me over thirty years ago one day when he told me to keep a look out for it. I said I would. Now here it was, the covering, the moon and sun and the earth arranged into a song, knowing nothing of the magic they made in the night. I let the book fall to my lap and sat back, my eyes steady on the shadow, the ground to which my chair and I were pinned, in which Hobbes lay curled, turning to cloth under us and spreading a giant cloak across the void. More wind blew like cutlery, a long, slow tinkling over Maine, what I would see if I rose up on wings over the forest, north to Quebec and east to Newfoundland, the bright foil of rivers, woods shook with frigid streams, wilderness run through with eagles, hawks, owls, bears, caribou, hungry herds gliding over the stones, the expanse of mountains and ice, roaming from night into day into night past wet towns nursed in valleys, the wide St. Lawrence salmon spearing ocean miles and river currents with a compass set for the narrow pond of their birth.

I passed an hour going from the clearing to the kitchen and back, more sherry, more music, more wood. And all the while the shadow passed across the moon until the reflected light dimmed to the color of paper, and then stone gray, and then burnt wood. And then there was no more in and out, and I was sitting in the big chair in the yard, arched for viewing through the trees with the pillow at my neck, the pipe in one hand, the book on my lap, the coffee in the other. Look at the hole in the sky, I thought, that was no giant glittering star in the night leading no men to their king. I waited, watching the faint stars find their places as the sun went behind the earth with all its light and switched off the moon.

When I felt the rushing through the woods behind me scurrying along the trails, I thought the whole world was sweeping itself clean in the vacuum, a piece of airless lightless space drenched down through the atmosphere. But it was just the snow wind again, this time reaching as far as the yard, and the first drops fell from the sky, from where I do not know, I saw no cloud. I was warm enough with the blanket and the coat, the gloves, and I wanted nothing on my head.

The truth was that I had lost track of the clock. I felt suspended in time not my own, not my choosing, a place I fell into by some omission or error, and grew. I might have risen then in my chair and be blown to the right time, backwards to an age I could breathe in, where my all waiting was right, a living place and pace, wine and hot meadows spread out under steeple bells.

Sitting in the chair, I watched the moon go a damp orange, then some blood seeped into it: and there it stayed, the true face of the moon, its true art, that cold, red flesh, a gunshot wound hung up in the night.

I watched it till I was so tired I had to close my eyes for a bit.

I had no logic, no excuse, no dreams that drove me to act or conjured a different man in me: every part

of the last few days, everything I had done and not
done, was my doing and mine alone. He was my friend,
and I loved him. That is all of it.

When I woke, the cup had fallen, the book too,
but the pipe still lay in my fingers. My ears were stones
rubber-banded in skin, my lips and nose sore and numb
at the same time. The moon had moved to the right and
found its light, and the sky had collapsed, a good few
inches of more snow fallen already, snow white-hot
with light, snow on my coat, snow down one boot
where the pants went inside, my sock drenched. Still I
wanted to stay, to wait for morning, to cover myself and
sleep the night out, but the fire was out for sure, and I
wondered idly about the time.

I carried everything inside, the chair last, and
resuscitated the flames. I watered the plants, stood
briefly in my bedroom, bending over the mattress on
the box springs, so much of my life spent unconscious
there. The clothes in the closet were few, a couple of
summer shirts. They could stay. An extra pair of summer
shoes. Best leave them here. I turned the gramophone
off and stored the record.

Since the cut in my shoulder was seeping red, I
looked for some calendula in the bathroom cupboard.
I opened the window, peered out then, and heard the
hiss of dead brittle leaves. I heard the sound as if a name
was being spoken, but the forest did not have a word for

itself that I knew. And what was I to call myself now in any case? To the woods, I was doubtless a wound living in a clearing, a patch of infection.

I passed the books, so many books, and wondered how they would fare without a fire. Now they would all be cold books, if they stayed together. I stood by the chair and placed my grandfather's pipe on one armrest, *The Winter's Tale* on the other, then stepped out past the porch and glanced again at the grave, wondered if another Hobbes would grow in the spring, and who would be there to see it if one did. I did not care to be there: I should be wiped away, erased like pencil, cleaned like wood dust from the grate. They'll have plenty to say now. What I wanted to say to that man as he walked ahead of me in the woods was that I didn't have feeling where I should and too much where I shouldn't. You keep away from men like me and you'll be alright in life.

I meant to say that to him, but it never came up.

Five young deer ran in the moonlight between the trees. I saw their eyes shine as they passed the cabin, bunching briefly before loosening into a quick trot, an accordion of hooves bounding through the downy white.

I don't know why but I waited a while watching the woods from the flowerbeds, as if Claire was going to come again out of the snow, for I had never figured how a woman who lived all those miles away in St. Agatha had ever walked out of these woods by accident.

★ ★ ★

But I did not have the time. I hoisted the rifle and began walking, leaving the two bullets remaining in the clip on the off chance I met Troy in the woods and he looked at me or had anything to say. He was wandering somewhere still, I guessed. I looked back from the edge of the clearing, remembering again, knowing again, and leaving for the first time everything my father knew. Although it was dark, I was familiar with the way and the light was good above me; once I reached the paved road it was only those twelve miles to Fort Kent. I would stay off the road and be there by dawn.

It being early morning on a Sunday, the police station would have one man on duty, it would be brightly lit and most likely warm, and somewhere in that building a hot cup of tea might be found, and we could talk for a while until some others came to take the details, driving straight from their beds maybe, running to their gates in long coats, from late fireplaces, from bottles. All this was clear in my mind as I took the dirt road with the Enfield. I saw the living flowers, my living father and Hobbes, and kept them firmly before me, but when I glanced again after only a minute the trees had closed in around and the cabin was lost to view.

ACKNOWLEDGMENTS

I want to thank my agent, Jin Auh; my editor, David Shoemaker, for his unwavering confidence in this novel; my friend and neighbor Doug Swanson, whose farm and dog inspired the story; and the following, who read the manuscript and told me what they thought of it: Richard Donovan, Sara Kallenbach, Graham Lewis, Tim McCarthy, Christina Nalty, and Jay Prefontaine. Martin Pegler's *Out of Nowhere* provided an excellent history of sniping. I found most of my lead character's Elizabethan vocabulary in David Crystal and Ben Crystal's *Shakespeare's Words: A Glossary and Language Companion*.